P9-EBY-222

ANOTHER FINE MYTH...

by
ROBERT ASPRIN

Edited and illustrated by Polly and Kelly Freas
Starblaze Editions • Donning • Norfolk • 1978

Other titles in this series:

Myth Conceptions
Myth Directions
Hit or Myth
Another Fine Myth is one of the many fantasy and science fiction titles published by The Donning Company/Publishers. For a complete listing of our titles, please write to the address below. Please include $1.00 for postage and handling.

Copyright © **1978 by Robert L. Asprin**
All rights reserved, including the right to reproduce this work in any form whatsoever without permission in writing from the publisher, except for brief passages in connection with a review. For information, write:

    The Donning Company/Publishers,
    5659 Virginia Beach Boulevard,
    Norfolk, Virginia 23502

Library of Congress Cataloging in Publication Data:

Asprin, Robert.

    Another fine myth.
    SUMMARY: After a magician's death, his apprentice, who is a thief, experiences a variety of adventures via a short-circuited dimension jumper.

    [1. Fantasy] I. Freas, Frank Kelly, 1922-
II. Title.
PZ4.A84123AN [PS3551.S6] 813'.5'4 [Fic] 78-2630
ISBN 0-915442-54-X

10 9 8 7 6 5

Printed in the United States of America.

This book is dedicated to

Bork The Indestructible
(Known to lesser mortals as George Hunt)

*whose gruff but loyal friendship has seen me through
many crises in the past...and probably in the future!*

ANOTHER
FINE
MYTH···

For the Dunn Under Show —

with best wishes

Robert Asprin 4/8/9

Chapter One:

"There are things on heaven and earth, Horatio, Man was not meant to know."

HAMLET

One of the few redeeming facets of instructors, I thought, is that occasionally they can be fooled. It was true when my Mother taught me to read, it was true when my Father tried to teach me to be a farmer, and it's true now when I'm learning magik.

"You haven't been practicing!" Garkin's harsh admonishment interrupted my musings.

"I have too!" I protested. "It's just a difficult exercise."

As if in response, the feather I was levitating began to tremble and wobble in midair.

"You aren't concentrating!" he accused.

"It's the wind," I argued. I wanted to add "from your loud mouth," but didn't dare. Early in our lessons Garkin had demonstrated his lack of appreciation for cheeky apprentices.

"The wind," he sneered, mimicking my voice. "Like this, dolt!"

My mental contact with the object of my concentration was interrupted as the feather darted suddenly toward the ceiling. It jarred to a halt as if it had become imbedded in something, though it was still a foot from the wooden beams, then slowly rotated to a horizontal plane. Just as slowly it rotated on its axis, then swapped ends and began to glide around an invisible circle like a leaf caught in an eddy.

I risked a glance at Garkin. He was draped over his chair, feet dangling, his entire attention apparently devoted to devouring a leg of roast lizard-bird, a bird I had snared I might add. Concentration indeed!

He looked up suddenly and our eyes met. It was too late to look away so I simply looked back at him.

"Hungry?" His grease-flecked salt and pepper beard was suddenly framing a wolfish grin. "Then show me how much you've been practicing."

It took me a heartbeat to realize what he meant; then I looked up desperately. The feather was tumbling floorward, a bare shoulder-height from landing. Forcing the sudden tension from my body, I reached out with my mind...gently...form a pillow...don't knock it away....

The feather halted a scant two hand-spans from the floor.

I heard Garkin's low chuckle, but didn't allow it to break my concentration. I hadn't let the feather touch the floor for three years, and it wasn't going to touch now.

Slowly I raised it until it floated at eye level. Wrapping my mind around it, I rotated it on its axis, then enticed it to swap ends. As I led it through the exercise, its movement was not as smooth or sure as when Garkin set his mind to the task, but it did move unerringly in its assigned course.

Although I had not been practicing with the feather, I had been practicing. When Garkin was not about or preoccupied with his own studies, I devoted most of my time to levitating pieces of metal— keys, to be specific. Each type of levitation had its own inherent problems. Metal was hard to work with because it was an inert material. The feather, having once been part of a living thing, was more responsive...too responsive. To lift metal took effort, to maneuver a feather required subtlety. Of the two, I preferred to work with metal. I could see a more direct application of that skill in my chosen profession.

"Good enough, lad. Now put it back in the book."

I smiled to myself. This part I had practiced, not because of its potential applications, but because it was fun.

The book was lying open on the end of the workbench. I brought the feather down in a long lazy spiral, allowing it to pass lightly across the pages of the book and up in a swooping arc, stopped it, and brought it back. As it approached the book the second time, I disengaged part of my mind to dart ahead to the book. As the feather crossed the pages, the book snapped shut like the jaws of a hungry predator, trapping the missile within its grasp.

"Hmmmm..." intoned Garkin, "a trifle showy, but effective."

"Just a little something I worked up when I was practicing," I said casually, reaching out with my mind for the other lizard-bird leg. Instead of floating gracefully to my waiting hand, however, it remained on the wooden platter as if it had taken root.

"Not so fast, my little sneak-thief. So you've been practicing, eh?" He stroked his beard thoughtfully with the half-gnawed bone in his hand.

"Certainly. Didn't it show?" It occurred to me that Garkin is not as easy to fool as it sometimes seems.

"In that case, I'd like to see you light your candle. It should be easy if you have been practicing as much as you claim."

"I have no objections to trying, but as you have said yourself so many times, some lessons come easier than others."

Although I sounded confident, my spirits sank as the large candle came floating to the work table in response to Garkin's summons. In four years of trying I was yet to be successful at this particular exercise. If Garkin was going to keep me from food until I was successful, I could go hungry for a long time.

"Say, uh, Garkin, it occurs to me I could probably concentrate better on a full stomach."

"It occurs to me that you're stalling."

"Couldn't I...."

"Now, Skeeve."

There was no swaying him once he used my proper name. That much I had learned over the years. Lad, Thief, Idiot, Turnip-Head, though derogatory, as long as he used one of these, his mind was still open. Once he reverted to using my proper name, it was hopeless. It is indeed a sorry state when the sound of your own name becomes a knell of doom.

Well, if there was no way around it, I'd just have to give it my best shot. For this there could be no half-effort or feigned concentration, I would have to use every ounce of my strength and skill to summon the power.

I studied the candle with a detached mind, momentarily blanking the effort ahead from my consciousness. The room, the cluttered workbench, Garkin, even my own hunger faded from view as I focused on the candle, though I had long since memorized its every feature.

It was stout, nearly six inches across to stabilize its ten-inch height. I had carved numerous mystic symbols into its surface, copied painstakingly from Garkin's books at his direction, though many of them were partially obliterated by hardened rivulets of wax. The candle had burned many long hours to light my studies, but it had always been lit from a taper from the cooking fire and not from my efforts.

Negative thought. Stop it.

I will light the candle this time. I will light it because there is no reason I should not.

Consciously deepening my breathing, I began to gather the power. My world narrowed further until all I was aware of was the curled, blackened wick of the candle.

I am Skeeve. My Father has a farmer's bond with the earth. My Mother was an educated woman. My teacher is a master magician. I am Skeeve. I will light this candle.

I could feel myself beginning to grow warm as the energies began to build within me. I focused the heat on the wick.

Like my Father, I tap the strength of the earth. The knowledge my Mother gave me is like a lens, enabling me to focus what I have gained. The wisdom of my teacher directs my efforts to those points of the universe most likely to yield to my will. I am Skeeve.

The candle remained unlit. There was sweat on my forehead now, and I was beginning to tremble with the effort. No that was wrong, I should not tense. Relax. Don't try to force it. Tenseness hinders the flow. Let the energies pass freely, serve as a passive conductor. I forced myself to relax, consciously letting the muscles in my face and shoulders go slack as I redoubled my efforts.

The flow was noticeably more intense now. I could almost see the energy streaming from me to my target. I stretched out a finger which focused the energies even more. The candle remained unlit.

I couldn't do it. Negative thought. Stop it. I am Skeeve. I will light the candle. My father....No. Negative thought. Do not rely on others for your strength. I will light the candle because I am Skeeve.

I was rewarded by a sudden surge of energy at the thought. I pursued it, growing heady with power. I am Skeeve. I am stronger than any of them. I escaped my father's attempts to chain me to a plow as he had my brother. My mother died from her idealism, but I used her teachings to survive. My teacher is a gullible fool who took a thief for an apprentice. I have beaten them all. I am Skeeve. I will light the candle.

I was floating now. I realized how my abilities dwarfed those around me. Whether the candle lit or not was inconsequential. I am Skeeve. I am powerful.

Almost contemptuously I reached out with my mind and touched the wick. A small bright ember appeared as if in answer to my will.

Startled, I sat up and blinked at the candle. As I did, the ember disappeared, leaving a small white plume of smoke to mark its departure. I realized too late I had broken concentration.

"Excellent, Lad!"

Garkin was suddenly beside me pounding my shoulder enthusiastically. How long he had been there I neither knew nor cared.

"It went out," I said plaintively.

"Never you mind that. You lit it. You have the confidence now. Next time it will be easy. By the stars, we'll make a magician of you yet. Here, you must be hungry."

I barely got my hand up in time to intercept the remaining lizard-bird leg before it smacked into my face. It was cold.

"I don't mind admitting I was beginning to despair, lad. What made that lesson so hard? Has it occurred to you you could use that spell to give you extra light when you're picking a lock or even to start a fire to serve as a diversion?"

"I thought about it, but extra light could draw unwanted attention. As for starting a diversion, I'd be afraid of hurting someone. I don't want to hurt anyone, just...."

I stopped, realizing what I was saying, too late. A heavy cuff from Garkin sent me sprawling off my stool.

"I thought so! You're still planning to be a thief. You want to use my magiks to steal!"

He was towering in his rage, but for once I stood my ground.

"What of it?" I snarled. "It beats starving. What's so good about being a magician, anyway? I mean, your life-style here gives me so much to look forward to."

I gestured at the cluttered room that was the entirety of the hut.

"Listen to the wolfling complain," Garkin sneered. "It was good enough for you when the winter drove you out of the woods to steal. 'It beats sleeping under a bush,' you said."

"And it still does. That's why I'm still here. But I'm not going to spend the rest of my life here. Hiding in a little hut in the woods is not my idea of a future to look forward to. You were living on roots and berries until I came along and started trapping meat for the fire. Maybe that's your idea of a wonderful life, Garkin, but it's not mine!"

We glared at each other for several long moments. Now that my anger was vented, I was more than a little afraid. While I had not had extensive experience in the field, I suspected that sneering at magicians was not the best way to ensure a long and healthy future.

Surprisingly enough, it was Garkin who gave ground first. He suddenly dropped his gaze and bowed his head, giving me a rare view of the unkempt mass of hair atop his head.

"Perhaps you're right, Skeeve," his voice was strangely soft. "Perhaps I have been showing you all the work of magik, but not the rewards. I constantly forget how surpressed magik is in these lands."

He raised his eyes to meet mine again, and I shivered at the impact. They were not angry, but deep within them burned a glow I had never seen before.

"Know you now, Skeeve, that all lands are not like this one, nor was I always as you see me now. In lands where magik is recognized instead of feared as it is here, it is respected and commissioned by those in power. There a skillful magician who keeps his wits about him can reap a hundred times the wealth you aspire to as a thief, and such power that...."

He broke off suddenly and shook his head as if to clear it. When he opened his eyes again, the glow I had seen burning earlier had died to an ember.

"But you aren't to be impressed by words, are you, lad? Come, I'll show you a little demonstration of some of the power you may one day wield—if you practice your lessons, that is."

The joviality in his voice was forced. I nodded my agreement in answer to that burning gaze. Truth to tell, I needed no demonstration. His soft, brief oration had awed me far more than any angry tirade or demonstration, but I did not wish to contradict him at this time.

I don't believe he actually noticed my response. He was already striding into the large pentagram permanently inscribed in the floor of the hut. As he walked, he gestured absentmindedly and the charred copper brazier scuttled forth from its place in the corner to meet him at the center of the pentagram.

I had time to reflect that perhaps it was that brazier that had first drawn me to Garkin. I remembered the first time I peered through the window of his hut seeking to identify and place objects of value for a later theft. I had seen Garkin as I have seen him so often since, pacing restlessly up and down the room, his nose buried in a book. It was a surprising enough sight as it was, for reading is not a common pastime in this area, but what captured my attention was the brazier. It hobbled about the room, following Garkin like an impatient puppy that was a little too polite to jump up on its master to get his attention. Then Garkin had looked up from his book, stared thoughtfully at his workbench; then, with a nod of decision, gestured. A small pot of unidentified content rose from the clutter and floated to his waiting hand. He caught it, referred to his book again, and poured out a dollop without looking up. Quick as a cat, the brazier scrambled under his hand and caught the dollop before it reached the floor. That had been my introduction to magik.

Something wrenched my attention back to the present. What was it? I checked Garkin's progress. No, he was still at work, half hidden by a floating cloud of vials and jars, mumbling as he occasionally plucked one from the air and added a bit of its contents to the brazier. Whatever he was working on, it promised to be spectacular.

Then I heard it again, a muffled step outside the hut. But that was impossible! Garkin always set the.... I began to search my memory. I could not recall Garkin setting the protective wards before he started to work. Ridiculous. Caution was the first and most important thing Garkin hammered into me, and part of caution was always setting wards before you started working. He couldn't have forgotten...but he had been rather intense and distracted.

I was still trying to decide if I should attempt to interrupt Garkin's work when he suddenly stepped back from the brazier. He fixed me with his gaze, and my warning died in my throat. This was not the time to impose reality on the situation. The glow was back in his eyes, stronger than before.

"Even demonstrations should give a lesson," he intoned. "Control, Skeeve. Control is the mainstay of magik. Power without control is a disaster. That is why you practice with a feather though you are able to move much larger and heavier objects. Control. Even your meager powers would be dangerous unless controlled, and I will not teach you more until you have learned that control."

He carefully stepped out of the pentagram.

"To demonstrate the value of control, I will now summon forth a demon, a being from another world. He is powerful, cruel, and vicious, and would kill us both if given the chance. Yet despite this, we need not fear him because he will be controlled. He will be unable to harm us or anything else in this world as long as he is contained within that pentagram. Now watch, Skeeve. Watch and learn."

So saying, he turned once more to the brazier. He spread his hands, and as he did, the five candles at the points of the pentagram sprang to life and the lines of the pentagram began to glow with an eerie blue light. Silence reigned for several minutes, then he began to chant in a low mumble. A thread of smoke appeared from the brazier, but instead of rising to the ceiling, it poured onto the floor and began to form a small cloud that seethed and pulsed. Garkin's chanting was louder now, and the cloud grew and darkened. The brazier was almost obscured from view, but there...in the depths of the cloud...something was taking shape....

"Isstvan sends his greetings, Garkin!"

I nearly jumped out of my skin at the words. They came from inside the hut, but not inside the pentagram! I whirled toward their source. A figure was standing just inside the door, blinding in a glowing gold cloak. For a mad moment I thought it was the demon answering Garkin's summons. Then I saw the crossbow. It was a man, alright, but the crossbow, cocked and loaded in his hand, did little for my peace of mind.

Garkin did not even turn to look.

"Not now, you fool!" he snarled.

"It has been a long hunt, Garkin," the man continued as if he hadn't heard. "You've hidden yourself well, but did you really hope to escape...."

"You dare!?!" Garkin spun from his work, towering in his rage.

The man saw Garkin's face now, saw the eyes, and his face contorted in a grotesque mask of fear. Reflexively, he loosed the bolt from his crossbow, but too late. I did not see what Garkin did, things were happening too fast, but the man suddenly disappeared in a sheet of flame. He shrieked in agony and fell to the floor. The flame disappeared as suddenly as it had come, leaving only the smoldering corpse as evidence it had existed at all.

I remained rooted to the spot for several moments before I could move or even speak.

"Garkin," I said at last, "I...Garkin!"

Garkin's form was a crumpled lump on the floor. I was at his side in one bound, but I was far too late. The crossbow bolt protruded with silent finality from his chest. Garkin had given me my last lesson.

As I stooped to touch his body, I noticed something that froze my blood in its veins. Half-hidden by his form was the extinguished candle from the north point of the pentagram. The lines were no longer glowing blue. The protective spell was gone.

With agonizing effort, I raised my head and found myself gazing into a pair of yellow eyes, flecked with gold, that were not of this world.

Chapter Two:

"Things are not always as they seem."
MANDRAKE

Once, in the woods, I found myself face to face with a snake-cat. On another occasion, I encountered a spider-bear. Now, faced with a demon, I decided to pattern my behavior after that which had saved me in the aforementioned situations. I froze. At least, in hindsight, I like to think it was a deliberate, calculated act.

The demon curled its lips back, revealing a double row of needle-sharp teeth.

I considered changing my chosen course of action; I considered fainting.

The demon ran a purple tongue over his lips and began to slowly extend a taloned hand toward me. That did it! I went backward, not in a catlike graceful bound, but scrabbling on all fours. It's surprising how fast you can move that way when properly inspired. I managed to build up a substantial head of steam before I crashed head-first into the wall.

"Gaahh...." I said. It may not seem like much, but at the time it was the calmest expression of pain and terror I could think of.

At my outburst, the demon seemed to choke. Several ragged shouts erupted, then he began to laugh. It wasn't a low menacing laugh, but the wholehearted enthusiastic laughter of someone who has just seen something hysterically funny.

I found it both disquieting and annoying. Annoying because I had a growing suspicion I was the source of his amusement; disquieting because...well...he was a demon and demons are...."

"Cold, vicious, and bloodthirsty," the demon gasped as if he had read my thoughts. "You really bought the whole line, didn't you, kid?"

"I beg your pardon?" I said because I couldn't think of anything else to say.

"Something wrong with your ears? I said 'cold, vicious....'"

"I heard you. I meant what did you mean."

"What I meant was that you were scared stiff, by a few well chosen words from my esteemed colleague, I'll wager." He jerked a thumb at Garkin's body. "Sorry for the dramatics. I felt a touch of comic relief was necessary to lighten an otherwise tragic moment."

"Comic relief?"

"Well, actually, I couldn't pass up the opportunity. You should have seen your face."

He chuckled to himself as he strode out of the pentagram and began leisurely inspecting the premises.

"So this is Garkin's new place, huh? What a dump. Who would have thought he'd come to this?"

To say I was perplexed would be an understatement. I wasn't sure how a demon should act, but it wasn't like this.

I could have bolted for the door, but I did not seem to be in immediate danger. Either this strange being meant me no harm, or he was confident of his ability to stop me even if I tried to flee. For the sake of my nervous system, I decided to assume the former.

The demon continued to inspect the hut, while I inspected him. He was humanoid; that is, he had two arms, two legs, and a head. He was short but powerfully built, a bit broader across the shoulders than a man, and heavily muscled, but he wasn't human. I mean, you don't see many hairless humans with dark green scales covering their body and pointed ears lying flat against their head.

I decided to risk a question.

"Ah, excuse me."

"Yeah, kid?"

"Um, you *are* a demon, aren't you?"

"Huh? Oh, yeah, I guess you could say I am."

"Well, if you don't mind my asking, why don't you act like a demon?"

The demon shot me a disgusted look, then turned his head heavenward in a gesture of martyrdom.

"Everybody's a critic. Tell ya' what, kid, would you be happier if I tore your throat out with my teeth?"

"Well, no, but...."

"For that matter, who are you, anyway? Are you an innocent bystander, or did you come with the assassin?"

"I'm with him," I hastened to reply, pointing a shaky finger at Garkin's body. That bit about tearing my throat out had me on edge again. "Or at least I was. Garkin. The one who summoned...him!...I'm...I was his student."

"No kiddin'? Garkin's apprentice?" He began advancing toward me, reaching out a hand, "Pleased ta...what's wrong?"

As he moved toward me, I had started backing away from him. I tried to do it casually, but he had noticed.

"Well...it's...you *are* a demon."

"Yeah. So?"

"Um...well, demons are supposed to be...."

"Hey, relax, kid. I don't bite. Look, I'm an old buddy of Garkin's."

"I thought you said you were a demon?"

"That's right. I'm from another dimension. A dimension traveler, or demon for short. Get it?"

"What's a dimension?"

The demon scowled.

"Are you sure you're Garkin's apprentice? I mean, he hasn't told you anything at all about dimensions?"

"No," I answered. "I mean, yes, I'm his apprentice, but he never said anything about the demon-suns."

"That's dimensions," he corrected. "Well, a dimension is another world, actually one of several worlds, existing simultaneously with this one, but on different planes. Follow me?"

"No," I admitted.

"Well, just accept that I'm from another world. Now, in that world, I'm a magician just like Garkin. We had an exchange program going where we could summon each other across the barrier to impress our respective apprentices."

"I thought you said you were a demon," I said suspiciously.

"I *am*! Look, kid. In my world, you'd be a demon, but at the current moment I'm in yours, so I'm a demon."

"I thought you said you were a magician."

"I don't believe this!" The demon made his angry appeal to the heavens. "I'm standing here arguing with some twerp of an apprentice....Look, kid."

He fixed me with his gaze again.

"Let me try it this way. Are you going to shake my hand, or am I going to rip your heart out?"

Since he put it that way...I mean, for a minute there, when he lost his temper and started shouting, he sounded just like Garkin. It gave credibility to his claim of friendship with my ex-teacher. I took his extended hand and shook it cautiously.

"I'm....My name is Skeeve."

His grip was cold, but firm. So firm in fact that I found it impossible to reclaim my hand as rapidly as I would have liked.

"Pleased ta meetcha, kid. I'm Aahz."

"Oz?"

"No relation."

"No relation to what?" I asked, but he was examining the room again.

"Well, there's certainly nothing here to arouse the greedy side of his fellow beings. Early primitive, enduring, but not particularly sought after."

"We like it," I said, rather stiffly. Now that I was over being scared, I didn't like the sneer in his voice. The hut wasn't much and I certainly wasn't overly fond of it, but I resented his criticism.

"Don't get your back up, kid." Aahz said easily. "I'm looking for a motive, that's all."

"Motive?"

"A reason for someone to off old Garkin. I'm not big on vengeance, but he was a drinking buddy of mine and it's got my curiosity up."

He broke off his inspection of the room to address me directly.

"How about you, kid? Can you think of anything? Any milkmaids he's seduced or farmers he's cheated? You've got an interest in this too, you know. You might be the next target."

"But the guy who did it is dead." I gestured to the charred lump by the door. "Doesn't that finish it?"

"Wake up, kid. Didn't you see the gold cloak? That was a professional assassin. Somebody hired him, and that somebody would hire another one."

A chill ran down my spine. I hadn't really thought of that. I began to search my memory for a clue.

"Well...he said Isstvan sent him."

"What's an Isstvan?"

"I don't...wait a minute. What do you mean, I might be the next target?"

"Neat, huh?" Aahz was holding up the gold cloak. "Lined, and completely reversible. Always wondered how come no one noticed them until they were ready to pounce."

"Aahz...."

"Hmmm? Oh, didn't mean to scare you. It's just if someone's declared open season on magicians in general or Garkin specifically, you might have some....Hello, what's this?"

"What's what?" I asked, trying to get a look at what he had found.

"This," he said, holding his prize aloft. "It seems I'm not the only demon about."

It was a head, apparently the assassin's. It was badly charred, with bone showing in several places. My natural revulsion at the sight was compounded by several obvious features. The chin and ears of the head were unnaturally pointed, and there were two short, blunt, horns protruding from the forehead.

"A devil!" I exclaimed in horror.

"A what? Oh, a Deveel. No, it's not from Deva, it's from Imper. An Imp. Didn't Garkin teach you anything?"

"Come again?" I asked, but Aahz was busy scowling at the head.

"The question is, who would be crass enough to hire an Imp for an assassin? The only one I can think of is Isstvan, but that's impossible."

"But that's who did it. Don't you remember? I told you...."

"I thought you said 'Isstvan.'"

"I did! Wait a minute. What did you say?"

"I said Isstvan. Can't you tell the difference?"

"No," I admitted.

"Hmmm...must be too subtle for the human ear to detect. Oh, well. No matter. This changes everything. If Isstvan is up to his old tricks there's no time to lose. Hey! Wait a minute. What's this?"

"It's a crossbow," I observed.

"With heat-seeking armor piercing quarrels? Is that the norm in this world?"

"Heat-seeking...."

"Never mind, kid. I didn't think so. Well, that tears it. I'd better check this out quick."

He began to stride into the pentagram. I suddenly realized he was preparing to leave.

"Hey! Wait a minute! What's going on?"

"It would take too long to explain, kid. Maybe I'll see you again sometime."

"But you said I might be a target!"

"Yeah, well, that's the way it crumbles. Tell ya what. Start running and maybe they won't find you until it's over."

My head was awhirl. Things were happening far too fast for clear thought. I still didn't know what or who the demon was or if I should trust him, but I did know one thing. He was the nearest thing to an ally I had in a situation where I was clearly outclassed.

"Couldn't you help me?"

"No time. I've got to move."

"Couldn't I come with you?"

"You'd just get in the way, maybe even get me killed."

"But without you, I'll be killed!"

I was getting desperate, but Aahz was unimpressed.

"Probably not. Tell ya what, kid. I've really got to get going, but just to show you I think you'll survive, I'll show you a little trick you might use sometime. You see all this crud Garkin used to bring me across the barrier? Well, it's not necessary. Watch close and I'll show you how we do it when our apprentices aren't watching."

I wanted to shout, to make him stop and listen to me, but he had already started. He spread his arms at shoulder height, looked heavenward, took a deep breath, then clapped his hands.

Nothing happened.

Chapter Three:

"The only thing more reliable than magik is one's friends!"

MACBETH

Aahz scowled and repeated the gesture, a bit quicker this time. The scene remained unchanged.

I decided something was wrong.

"Is something wrong?" I asked politely.

"You'd better believe there's something wrong," Aahz snarled. "It's not working."

"Are you sure you're doing it right?"

"Yes, I'm sure I'm doing it right, just like I've been sure the last fifty times I did it!"

He was starting to sound annoyed.

"Can you...."

"Look, kid. If I knew what was wrong, I'd have fixed it already. Now, just shut up and let me think!"

He sank down to sit cross-legged in the center of the pentagram where he began sketching vague patterns in the floor as he mumbled darkly to himself. I wasn't sure if he was trying some alternate incantation or was simply thinking hard, but decided it would be unwise to ask. Instead, I used the time to organize my scrambled thoughts.

I still wasn't sure if Aahz was a threat to me or if he was my only possible salvation from a greater threat. I mean, by this time I was pretty sure he was kidding about ripping my heart out, but that's the sort of thing one wants to be very sure of. One thing I had learned for certain, there was more to this magik stuff than floating feathers around.

"That's got to be it!"

Aahz was on his feet again, glaring at Garkin's body.

"That ill-begot son of a wombat!"

"What's a wombat?" I asked, then immediately wished I hadn't. The mental image that sprang into my mind was so horrifying I was sure I didn't want details. I needn't have worried. Aahz was not about to take time to answer me.

"Well, it's a pretty crummy joke. That's all I have to say."

"Um....What are you talking about, Aahz?"

"I'm talking about Garkin! He did this to me. If I thought it would go this far, I would have turned him into a goat-fish when I had the chance."

"Aahz....I still don't...."

I stopped. He had ceased his ranting and was looking at me. I shrank back reflexively before I recognized the snarl as his smile. I liked it better when he was raving.

"I'm sorry, Skeeve," he purred. "I guess I haven't been very clear."

I was growing more uneasy by the minute. I wasn't used to having people, much less demons, being nice to me.

"Um....That's okay. I was just wondering...."

"You see, the situation is this. Garkin and I have been...playing little jokes on each other for some time now. It started one time when we were drinking and he stiffed me with the bill. Well, the next time I summoned him, I brought him in over a lake and he had to do his demon act armpit deep in water. He got even by...well, I won't bore you with details, but we've gotten in the habit of putting each other in awkward or embarrassing situations. It's really very childish, but quite harmless. But this time...." Aahz's eyes started to narrow, "But this time the old frog-kisser's gone too...I mean, it seems to have gotten a little out of hand. Don't you agree?"

He bared his fangs at me again in a smile. I wanted very badly to agree with him, but I didn't have the foggiest idea what he was talking about.

"You still haven't told me what's wrong."

"What's wrong is that stinking slime-monger took away my powers!" he roared, forgetting his composure. "I'm blocked! I can't do a flaming thing unless he removes his stupid prankish spell and he can't 'cause he's dead! Now do you understand me, fly-bait?"

I made up my mind. Savior or not, I'd rather he went back where he came from.

"Well, if there was anything I could do...."

"There is, Skeeve, my boy." Aahz was suddenly all purrs and teeth again. "All you have to do is fire up the old cauldron or whatever and remove this spell. Then we can each go our separate ways and...."

"I can't do that."

"Okay, kid," his smile was a little more forced. "I'll stick around until you're on your feet. I mean, what are friends for?"

"That's not it."

"What do you want? Blood?" Aahz was no longer smiling. "If you're trying to hold me up, I'll...."

"You don't understand!" I interrupted desperately. "I can't do it because I can't do it! I don't know how!"

That stopped him.

"Hmm. That could be a problem. Well, tell you what. Instead of pulling the spell here, what say you just pop me back to my own dimension and I'll get someone there to take it off."

"I can't do that either. Remember, I told you I'd never even heard of...."

"Well, what *can* you do?!"

"I can levitate objects...well, small objects."

"And...." he encouraged.

"And...um...I can light a candle."

"Light a candle?"

"Well...almost."

Aahz sank heavily into a chair and hid his face in his hands for several minutes. I waited for him to think of something.

"Kid, have you got anything in this dump to drink?" he asked finally.

"I'll get you some water."

"I said something to drink, not something to wash in!"

"Oh. Yessir!"

I hastened to bring him a goblet of wine from the small keg Garkin kept, hoping he wouldn't notice the vessel wasn't particularly clean.

"What will this do? Will it help you put your powers back?"

"No. But it might make me feel a little better." He tossed the wine down in one swallow, and studied the goblet disdainfully. "Is this the biggest container you've got?"

I cast about the room desperately, but Aahz was way ahead of me.

He rose, strode into the pentagram, and picked up the brazier. I knew from past experience it was deceptively heavy, but he carried it to the keg as if it were weightless. Not bothering to empty out Garkin's concoction, he filled it to the brim and took a deep draught.

"Aah! That's better." he sighed.

I felt a little queasy.

"Well, kid," he said, sweeping me with an appraising stare, "it looks like we're stuck with each other. The set-up isn't ideal, but it's what we've got. Time to bite the bullet and play the cards we're dealt. You do know what cards are, don't you?"

"Of course," I said, slightly wounded.

"Good."

"What's a bullet?"

Aahz closed his eyes as if struggling against some inner turmoil.

"Kid," he said at last, "there's a good chance this partnership is going to drive one of us crazy. I would guess it will be me unless you can knock off the dum-dum questions every other sentence."

"But I can't understand half of what you're saying."

"Hmm. Tell ya what. Try to save up the questions and ask me all at one time once a day. Okay?"

"I'll try."

"Right. Now here's the situation as I see it. If Isstvan is hiring Imps for assassins...."

"What's an Imp?"

"Kid, will you give me a break?"

"I'm sorry, Aahz. Keep going."

"Right. Well...umm....It's happening!" he made his appeal to the heavens. I can't remember what I was saying!"

"Imps," I prompted.

"Oh! Right. Well, if he's hiring Imps and arming them with non-spec weapons, it can only mean he's up to his old tricks. Now since I don't have my powers, I can't get out of here to sound the alarm. That's where you come in, kid....Kid?"

He was looking at me expectantly. I found I could contain my misery no longer.

"I'm sorry, Aahz," I said in a small, pitiful voice I hardly recognized as my own. "I don't understand a single thing you've said."

I suddenly realized I was about to cry, and turned away hurriedly so he wouldn't see. I sat there, with tears trickling down my cheeks, alternately fighting the urge to wipe them away and wondering why I was concerned over whether or not a demon saw me crying. I don't know how long I stayed that way, but I was brought back to reality by a gentle hand on my shoulder, a cold, gentle hand.

"Hey, kid. Don't beat on yourself," Aahz's voice was surprisingly sympathetic. "It's not your fault if Garkin was tight with his secrets. Nobody expects you to have learned something you

18

were never taught, so there's no reason you should expect it either."

"I just feel so stupid," I said, not turning. "I'm not used to feeling stupid."

"You aren't stupid, kid. That much I know. Garkin wouldn't have taken you for an apprentice if you were stupid. If anybody here's stupid, it's me. I got so carried away with the situation, I forgot myself and tried talking to an apprentice as if he were a full blown magician. Now that's stupid."

I still couldn't bring myself to respond.

"Heck, kid." He gave my shoulder a gentle shake. "Right now you can do more magik than I can."

"But you know more."

"But I can't use it. You know, kid, that gives me an idea. With old Garkin dead there, you're kind of cut off. What say you sign on as my apprentice for a while. We'll take it from the top with me teaching you as if you were a new student who didn't know a thing. We'll take it step by step from the beginning. What da ya say?"

In spite of my gloom I felt my spirits lift. Like he said, I'm not stupid. I could recognize a golden opportunity when I saw one.

"Gee, that sounds great, Aahz."

"Then it's a deal?"

"It's a deal," I answered and stuck out my hand.

"What's that?" he snarled. "Isn't my word good enough for you?"

"But you said...."

"That's right. You're my apprentice now, and I don't go around shaking apprentices' hands."

I withdrew my hand. It occurred to me this alliance might not be all roses and song.

"Now as I was saying, here's what we've got to do about the current situation...."

"But I haven't had any lessons yet!"

"That's right. Here's your first lesson. When a crisis shapes up, you don't waste energy wishing for information or skills you haven't got. You dig in and handle it as best you can with what you've got. Now shut up while I fill you in on the situation...apprentice."

I shut up and listened. He studied me for a moment, then gave a small satisfied nod, took another gulp from the brazier and began.

"Now, you have a vague idea about other dimensions because I told you about them earlier. You also have first hand experience that magicians can open passages in the barriers between those dimensions. Well, different magicians use that power in different ways. Some of them, like Garkin, only use it to impress the yokels; summon a demon, visions of other worlds, that kind of schtick. But there are others whose motives are not so pure."

He paused to take another gulp of wine. Surprisingly, I felt no urge to interrupt with questions.

"Technology in different dimensions has progressed at different rates, as has magik. Some magicians use this to their own advantage. They aren't showmen, they're smugglers, buying and selling technology across the barriers for profit and power. Most of the inventors in any dimension are actually closet magicians."

I must have frowned without realizing it, but Aahz noted it and acknowledged it with a wink and a smirk.

"I know what you're thinking, Skeeve. It all sounds a little dishonest and unscrupulous. Actually, they're a fairly ethical bunch. There's a set of unwritten rules called the Smugglers Code they adhere to pretty closely."

"Smugglers Code?" I asked, forgetting myself for a moment. Aahz didn't seem to mind this time.

"It's like the Mercenaries Code, but less violent and more profitable. Anyway, as an example, one item in that code states you cannot bring an 'invention' into a dimension that is too far in advance of that dimension's technology, like bringing guided missiles into a longbow culture or lasers into a flint and powder era."

I kept my silence with great difficulty.

"As I've said, most magicians adhere to the code fairly closely, but once in a while a bad one crops up. That brings us to Isstvan."

I got a sudden chill at the sound of that name. Maybe there *was* something different in the way Aahz pronounced it.

"Some say Isstvan isn't playing with a full deck. I think he's been playing with his wand too much. But whatever the reason, somewhere he's gotten it into his head he wants to rule the dimensions, all of them. He's tried it before, but we got wind of it in time and a bunch of us teamed up to teach him a lesson in manners. As a matter of fact, that's when I first met Garkin there."

He gestured with the brazier and slopped a bit of wine on the floor. I began to doubt his sobriety, but his voice seemed steady enough as he continued.

"I thought he had given the thing up after his last drubbing. We even gave him a few souvenirs to be sure he didn't forget. Then this thing pops up. If he's hiring cross-dimension help and arming them with advance technology weapons, he's probably trying to do it again."

"Do what?"

"I just told you. Take over the dimensions."

"I know, but how? I mean, how does what he does in this dimension help him rule the others?"

"Oh, that. Well, each dimension has a certain amount of power that can be channeled or converted into magik. Different dimensions have different amounts, and each dimension's power is divided up or shared by the magicians of that dimension. If he can succeed in controlling or killing the other magicians in this dimension, he can use its entire magical energy to attack another dimension. If he succeeds in winning there, he has the power from two dimensions to attack a third, and so on. As you can see, the longer he keeps his plot moving, the stronger he gets and the harder he'll be to stop."

"I understand now," I said, genuinely pleased and enthusiastic.

"Good. Then you understand why we've got to stop him."

I stopped being pleased and enthusiastic.

"We? You mean us? You and me?"

"I know it's not much of a force, kid, but like I said, it's all we've got."

"I think I'd like a little of that wine now."

"None of that, kid. You're in training now. You're going to need all the practice time you can get if we're going to stop Isstvan. Bonkers or not, he's no slouch when it comes to magik."

"Aahz," I said slowly, not looking up. "Tell me the truth. Do you think there's a chance you can teach me enough magik that we'll have a chance of stopping him?"

"Of course, kid. I wouldn't even try if we didn't have a chance. Trust me."

I wasn't convinced, and from the sound of his voice, neither was he.

Chapter Four:

"Careful planning is the key to safe and swift travel."

ULYSSES

"Hmmm...Well, it's not a tailored jump-suit, but it will have to do."

We had been trying to outfit Aahz in a set of clothes and he was surveying the results in a small dark mirror we had found, turning it this way and that to catch his reflection piecemeal.

"Maybe if we could find some other color than this terrible brown."

"That's all we've got."

"Are you sure?"

"Positive. I have two shirts, both brown. You're wearing one, and I'm wearing the other."

"Hmmm...." he said, studying me carefully. "Maybe I would look better in the lighter brown. Oh, well, we can argue that out later."

I was curious as to his attention to his appearance. I mean, he couldn't be planning on meeting anyone. The sight of a green, scaly demon would upset most of the locals no matter what he was wearing. For the time being, however, I deemed it wisest to keep quiet and humor him in his efforts.

Actually, the clothes fit him fairly well. The shirt was a bit short in the sleeves due to the length of his arms, but not too because I was taller than him which made up for most of the difference. We had had to cut off some of the trouser legs to cover for his shorter legs, but they, like the body of the shirt, were not too tight. I had made the clothes myself originally, and they tended to be a bit baggy, or at least they were on me. Tailoring is not my forte.

He was also wearing Garkins' boots, which fitted him surprisingly well. I had raised minor protest at this, until he pointed out Garkin had no further use for them but we did. Pragmatism, he called it. Situational ethics. He said it would come in handy if I was serious about becoming a magician.

"Hey, kid!" Aahz's voice interrupted my thoughts. He seemed to be occupied rummaging through the various chests and cupboards of the hut. "Don't you have anything here in the way of weapons?"

"Weapons?"

"Yeah, you know, the things that killed old Garkin there. Swords, knives, bows, stuff like that."

"I know what they are. I just wasn't expecting you to be interested in them, that's all."

"Why not?"

"Well...I thought you said you were a magician."

"We aren't going to go through *that* again, are we, kid? Besides, what's that got to do with weapons?"

"It's just that I've never known a magician who used weapons other than his powers."

"Really? How many magicians have you known?"

"One," I admitted.

"Terrific. Look, kid, if old Garkin didn't want to use weapons, that's his problem. Me, I want some. If you'll notice, Garkin is dead."

It was hard to argue wih logic like that.

"Besides," he continued, "do you really want to take on Isstvan and his pack with nothing but your magik and my agility going for us?"

"I'll help you look."

We went to work rummaging for weapons, but aside from the crossbow that had killed Garkin, we didn't find much. One of the chests yielded a sword with a jewel-encrusted handle, and we discovered two knives, one white handled and one black handled, on Garkin's workbench. Aside from those, there was nothing even remotely resembling a fighting utensil in the hut. Aahz was not overjoyed.

"I don't believe this. A sword with a cruddy blade, bad balance, and phony jewels in the handle and two knives that haven't been sharpened since they were made. Anybody who keeps weapons like this should be skewered."

"He was."

"True enough. Well, if that's all we've got, that's what we'll have to use."

He slung the sword on his hip and tucked the white handled knife into his belt. I thought he would give me the other knife, but instead he stooped down and secured it in his boot.

"Don't I get one?"

"Can you use it?"

"Well...."

He resumed his task. I had a small knife I used to skin small game tucked in my own belt inside my shirt. Even to my inexperienced eye it was of better quality than the two Aahz had just appropriated. I decided not to bring it to his attention.

"Okay, kid. Where did the old man keep his money?"

I showed him. One of the stones in the fireplace was loose and there was a small leather pouch hidden behind it. He peered at the coins suspiciously as they poured into his palm.

"Check me on this, kid. Copper and silver aren't worth much in this dimension, right?"

"Well, silver's sorta valuable, but it's not worth as much as gold."

"Then what's with this chicken-feed? Where's the real money?"

"We never really had much."

"Come off it...I haven't met a magician yet who didn't have a bundle socked away. Just because he never spent any of it doesn't mean he doesn't have it. Now think. Haven't you ever seen anything around that was gold or had gems?"

"Well, there are a few items, but they're protected by curses."

"Kid, think for a minute. If you were a doddering old wreck who couldn't fight your way out of a paper bag, how would you protect your treasures?"

"I don't know."

"Terrific. I'll explain while we gather it up."

In short order we had a modest heap of loot on the table, most of it items I had long held in awe. There was a gold statue of a man with the head of a lion, the Three Pearls of Kraul, a gold pendant in the shape of the sun with three of its rays missing, and a ring with a large jewel we took from Garkin's hand. Aahz held up the sun pendant.

"Now this is an example of what I mean. I suppose there's a story about what happened to the missing three rays?"

"Well," I began, "there was a lost tribe that worshipped a huge snake toad...."

"Skip it. It's an old dodge. What you do is take your gold to a craftsman and have him fashion it into something with a lot of small out-juttings like fingers or arms...." He held up the pendant. "...rays of sun. It gives you the best of two worlds.

"First, you have something mystical and supernatural, add a ghost story and no one will dare to touch it. Second, it has the advantage that if you need a little ready cash, you just break off a ray or an arm and sell it for the value of the gold. Instead of losing value, the price of the remaining item increases because of its mystical history, the strange circumstances under which it was torn asunder, purely fictional, of course."

Strangely enough, I was not surprised. I was beginning to wonder if anything Garkin had told me was true.

"Then none of these things have any real magical powers or curses?"

"Now, I didn't say that. Occasionally, you stumble across a real item, but they're usually few and far between."

"But how can you tell the real thing from a fake?"

"I take it that Garkin didn't teach you to see auras. Well, that figures. Probably was afraid you'd take his treasure and run. Okay, kid. Time for your first lesson. Have you ever day-dreamed? You know, just stared at something and let your mind wander?"

I nodded.

"Okay, here's what I want you to do. Scoot down in your chair until your head is almost level with the table. That's right. Comfortable? Fine. Now I want you to look across the table at the wall. Don't focus on it, just stare at it and let your mind wander."

I did as he said. It was hard not focusing on a specific point, so I set my mind to wandering. What to think about? Well, what was I thinking about when the candle almost lit. Oh yes. I am Skeeve. I am powerful and my power is growing daily. I smiled to myself. With the demon's aid, I would soon become a knowledgeable sorcerer. And that would just be the start. After that....

"Hey!" I said, sitting upright.

"What did you see?"

"It was... well, nothing, I guess."

"Don't give me a hard time, kid. What did you see?"

"Well, for a second there I thought I saw sort of a red glow around the ring, but when I looked at it squarely, it disappeared."

"The ring, eh? It figures. Well, that's it. The rest of the stuff should be okay."

He scraped the rest of the loot into a sack, leaving the ring on the table.

"What was it?"

"What? Oh, what you saw? That was an aura. Most people have them. Some places do, but it's a sure test to check if an item is truly magical. I'd be willing to bet that the ring is what old Garkin used to fry the assassin."

"Aren't we going to take it with us?"

"Do you know how to control it?"

"Well....no."

"Neither do I. The last thing we need is to carry around a ring that shoots fire. Particularly if we don't know how to activate it. Leave it. Maybe the others will find it and turn it on themselves."

He tucked the sack into his waistband.

"What others?" I prompted.

"Hmmm? Oh, the other assassins."

"What other assassins?" I was trying to be calm, but I was slipping.

"That's right. This is the first time you've tangled with them, isn't it? I would have thought Garkin...."

"Aahz, could you just tell me?"

"Oh! Sure, kid. Assassins never work alone. That's why they never miss. They work in groups of two to eight. There's probably a back-up team around somewhere. Realizing Isstvan's respect for Garkin, I'd guess he wouldn't send less than six out on an assignment like this, maybe even two teams."

"You mean all this time you've been fooling around with clothes and swords, there's been more assassins on the way?"

"Relax, kid. That's the back-up team. They'll be waiting aways off and won't move until tomorrow at the earliest. It's professional courtesy. They want to give this bozo room to maneuver. Besides, it's tradition that the assassin who actually does the deed gets first pick of any random booty lying around before the others show up to take even shares. Everyone does it, but it's considered polite to not notice some of the loot has been pocketed before the official split."

"How do you know so much about assassins, Aahz?"

"Went with one for a while...lovely lass, but she couldn't keep her mouth shut, even in bed. Sometimes I wonder if any profession really guards its secrets as closely as they claim."

"What happened?"

"With what?"

"With your assassin?"

"None of your business, kid." Aahz was suddenly brusque again. "We've got work to do."

"What are we going to do?"

"Well, first we bury the Imp. Maybe it will throw the others off our trail. With any luck, they'll think he grabbed all the loot and disappeared. It wouldn't be the first time."

"No, I mean after that. We're getting ready to travel, but where are we going?"

"Kid, sometimes you worry me. That isn't even magic. It's

common sense military action. First, we find Isstvan. Second, we appraise his strength. Third, we make our plans, and fourth, we execute them, and hopefully him."

"Um...Aahz, could we back up to one for a minute? Where are we going to find Isstvan?"

That stopped him.

"Don't you know where he is?"

"I never even heard his name before today."

We sat in silence staring at each other for a long time.

Chapter Five:

"Only constant and conscientious practice in the
Martial Arts will ensure a long and happy life."
B. LEE

"I think I've got it figured out, kid."

As Aahz spoke, he paused in honing his sword to inspect the edge. Ever since our trek began he had seized every opportunity to work on his weapons. Even when we simply paused to rest by a stream he busied himself working their edges or adjusting their balance. I felt I had learned more about weapons in the last week just watching him tinker than I had in my entire previous life.

"Figured what out?"

"Why people in this world are trained in weapons or magik, but not both!"

"How's that?"

"Well, two reasons I can see just offhand. First off, it's a matter of conditioning. Reflexes. You'll react the way you're trained. If you've been trained with weapons, you'll react to crisis with a weapon. If you're trained in magik, you'll react with magik. The problem is, if you're trained both ways, you'll hesitate, trying to make up your mind which to use, and probably get clobbered in the process. So to keep things simple, Garkin only trained you in magik. It's probably all he had been trained in himself."

I thought about it.

"That makes sense. What's the other reason?"

He grinned at me.

"Learning curve. If what you told me about life expectancy in this world is even vaguely accurate, and if you're any example of how fast people in this world learn, you only have time to learn one or the other."

"I think I prefer the first explanation."

He chortled to himself and went back to sharpening his sword.

Once his needling would have bothered me, but now I took it in stride. It seemed to be his habit to be critical of everything in our world, and me in particular. After a week of constant exposure to him, the only way I would worry is if he stopped complaining.

Actually I was quite pleased with my progress in magik. Under Aahz's tutelage, my powers were growing daily. One of the most valuable lessons I had learned was to draw strength directly from the earth. It was a matter of envisioning energy as a tangible force, like water, and drawing new energy up one leg and into my mind while releasing exhausted energy down the other leg and back into the earth. Already, I could completely recharge myself even after a hard day's walking just by standing motionless with my eyes closed for several minutes and effecting this energy exchange. Aahz, as always, was unimpressed. According to him, I should have been able to do the energy exchange while we were walking, but I didn't let his grumbling dampen my enthusiasm. I was learning, and at a faster pace than I had dreamed possible.

"Hey, kid. Fetch me a piece of wood, will you?"

I smiled to myself and looked around. About ten feet away was a small branch of deadwood about two feet long. I leisurely stretched out a finger and it took flight, floating gently across the clearing to hover in the air in front of Aahz.

"Not bad, kid," he acknowledged. Then his sword flashed out, cutting the branch into two pieces which dropped to the ground. He picked up one of the pieces and inspected the cut.

"Hmmm...there may be hope for this sword yet. Why did you let them fall?"

This last was directed at me.

"I don't know. I guess you startled me when you swung the sword."

"Oh, really?"

Suddenly he threw the stick at me. I yelped and tried to duck out of the way, but it bounced painfully off my shoulder.

"Hey! What was that for?"

"Call it an object lesson. You know you can control the stick because you just did it when you fetched it for me. So why did you duck out of the way? Why not just stop it with your magik?"

"I guess it never occurred to me. You didn't give me much time to think."

"Okay, so think! This time you know it's coming."

He picked up the second piece of wood and waited, grinning evilly, which with pointed teeth is easy. I ignored him, letting my mind settle; then I nodded that I was ready.

The stick struck me squarely in the chest.

"Ow!!" I commented.

"And there, my young friend, is the difference between classroom and field. Classroom is fine to let you know that things can be done and that you can do them, but in actual practice you will never be allowed the luxury of leisurely gathering your power, and seldom will you have a stationary target.

"Say, uh, Aahz. If you're really trying to build up my self-confidence, how come you always cut my legs out from under me every time I start thinking I'm getting someplace?"

He stood up, sheathing his sword.

"Self-confidence is a wonderful thing, kid, but not if it isn't justified. Someday we'll be staking one or both of our lives on your abilities, and it won't do us any good if you've been kidding yourself along. Now let's get down to work!"

"Um...have we got the time?"

"Relax, kid. Imps are tenacious, but they travel slow."

Our strategy upon leaving the hut had been simple. Lacking a specific direction for our search, we would trace the force lines of the world until we either found Isstvan or located another magician who would be able to steer us to him.

One might ask what force lines are. I did. Force lines, as Aahz explained them, are those paths of a world along which its energies flow most freely. In many ways, they are not unlike magnetic lines.

One might ask what magnetic lines are. I did. I will not quote Aahz's answer to that, but it was not information.

Anyway, force lines are a magician's ally and enemy. Those who would tap the energies of those lines usually set up residence on or near one of those lines. This makes it easier for them to draw upon the energies. It also makes it easier for their enemies to find them.

It was Aahz's theory that searching the force lines was how Garkin was located. It was therefore logical that we should be able to find Isstvan the same way.

Of course, I knew nothing of force lines or how to follow them, at least until Aahz taught me. It was not a difficult technique, which was fortunate as I had my hands full trying to absorb all the other lessons Aahz was deluging me with.

One simply closes ones eyes and relaxes, trying to envision a two-pointed spear in glowing yellows and reds suspended in mid-air. The intensity of the glow indicates the nearness to a force line; the direction of the points shows the flow of energies. Rather like the needle of a compass, whatever that is.

Once we had determined that Garkin had set up shop directly on a force line, as Aahz had suspected, and established direction of the flow of energies, we had another problem. Which way did we follow it?

The decision was doubly important as, if Aahz was correct, there would be a team of Imp assassins waiting in one direction, very probably in the direction we wanted to go.

We solved the problem by traveling one day's journey perpendicular to the force line, then for two days parallel to the line in our chosen direction, then returning to the line before continuing our journey. We hoped this would bypass the assassins entirely.

It worked, and it didn't.

It worked in that we didn't walk into an ambush. It didn't work in that now it seemed they were on our trail, though whether they were actually tracking us or merely following the force line back to Isstvan was unknown.

"I keep telling you, kid," Aahz insisted. "It's a good sign. It means we've chosen the right direction, and that we'll reach Isstvan ahead of his assassins' report."

"What if we're heading in the wrong direction?" I argued. "What if they're really following us? How long do we travel in this direction before we give up and admit it?"

"How long do you figure it will take for you to learn enough magik to stand up to a pack of Imp assassins armed with off-dimension weapons?"

"Let's get to work," I said firmly.

He looked around, and pointed to a gnarled fruit tree strewn round with windfalls across the clearing.

"Okay. Here's what I want you to do. Stare at the sky or contemplate your navel or something. Then when I give the word, use your power to grab one of those fruits and toss it to me."

I don't know how many hours we spent on that drill. It's more difficult than it sounds, mustering one's powers from a standing start. Just when I thought I had it down pat, Aahz switched tactics. He would engage in a conversation, deliberately leading me on, then would interrupt me in mid-sentence with his signal. Needless to say,I failed miserably.

"Relax, kid. Look, try it this way. Instead of mustering your power from scratch each time, create a small space inside yourself and store up some energy there. Just habitually keep that reserve squirreled away and ready to cover for you while you get set to level your big guns."

"What's a gun?"

"Never mind. Just build that reserve and we'll try it again."

With this extra bit of advice at my disposal the drill went noticeably better. Finally Aahz broke off the practice session and put me to work helping him with his knife practice. Actually I rather enjoyed this task. It entailed my using my powers to levitate one of the fruits and send it flying around the clearing until Aahz pegged a knife into it. As an extra touch of finesse, I would then extract the knife and float it back to him for another try. The exercise was monotonous, but I never tired of it. It seemed almost supernatural the way the shimmering, somersaulting sliver of steel would dart out to intercept the fruit as Aahz practiced first overhand, then underhand, now backhand.

"Stop it, Skeeve!"

Aahz's shout jolted me out of my reverie. Without thinking, I reached out with my mind and ... and the knife stopped in midair! I blinked, but held it there, floating a foot from the fruit which also hung suspended in place.

"Hel-lo! That's the stuff, Skeeve! Now there's something to have confidence in!"

"I did it!" I said, disbelieving my own eyes.

"You sure did! That little piece of magik will save your life someday."

Out of habit, I floated the knife back to him. He plucked it from the air and started to tuck it in his belt, then halted, cocking his head to one side.

"In the nick of time, too. Someone's coming."

"How can you tell?"

"Nothing special. My hearing's a bit better than yours is all. Don't panic. It isn't the Imps. Hooved beast from the sound of it. No wild animal moves in that straight a line, or that obviously."

"What did you mean, 'in the nick of time'? Aren't we going to hide?"

"Not this time." He grinned at me. "You're developing fast. It's about time you learned a new spell. We have a few days before whoever it is gets here."

"Days?"

Aahz was adapting rapidly to our dimension, but units of time still gave him trouble.

"Run through those time measurements again," he grumbled.

"In seconds, minutes, hours...."

"Minutes! We've got a few minutes."

"Minutes! I can't learn a new spell in a few minutes!"

"Sure you can. This one's easy. All you've got to do is disguise my features to look like a man."

"How do I do that?"

"The same way you do everything else, with your mind. First, close your eyes...close 'em...okay, now picture another face...."

All I could think of was Garkin, so I pictured the two faces side by side.

"Now move the new face over mine...and melt away or build up the necessary features. Like clay...just keep that in the back of your mind and open your eyes."

I looked, and was disappointed.

"It didn't work!"

"Sure it did."

He was looking in the dark mirror which he had fished from his belt pouch.

"But you haven't changed!"

"Yes it did. You can't see it because you cast the spell. It's an illusion, and since your mind knows the truth, it isn't fooled, but anyone else will be. Garkin, huh? Well, it'll do for now."

His identification of the new face took me aback.

"You can really see Garkin's face?"

"Sure, want to look?"

He offered the mirror and grinned. It was a bad joke. One of the first things we discovered about his dubious status in this world was that while he could see himself in mirrors, nobody from our world could. At least I couldn't.

I could now hear the sounds of the rider coming.

"Aahz, are you sure...."

"Trust me, kid. There's nothing to worry about."

I was worried. The rider was in view now. He was a tall muscular man with the look of a warrior about him. This was reinforced by the massive war unicorn he was riding, laden with weapons and armor.

"Hey, Aahz. Shouldn't we...."

"Relax, kid. Watch this."

He stepped forward, raising his arm.

"Hello, Stranger! How far to the next town?"

The man veered his mount toward us. He half raised his arm in greeting, then suddenly stiffened. Heaving forward, he squinted at Aahz, then drew back in terror.

"By the Gods! A demon!"

Chapter Six:

"Attention to detail is the watchword for gleaning information from an unsuspecting witness."
INSP. CLEUSEAU

The warrior's terror did not immobilize him long. In fact, it didn't immobilize him at all! No sooner did he make his discovery then he took action. Strangely enough, the action was to lean back in his saddle and begin rummaging frantically through one of his saddlebags, a precarious position at best.

Apparently I was not the only one to notice the instability of his pose. Aahz sprang forward with a yell, waving his arms in the unicorn's face. Being a reasonable creature, the unicorn reared and bolted, dumping the warrior on his head.

"By the Gods!" he bellowed, trying to untangle himself from the ungraceful heap of arms and weapons. "I've killed men for less!"

I decided that if his threat was to be avoided, I should take a personal hand in the matter. Reaching out with my mind, I seized a fist-sized rock and propelled it forcefully against his unhelmeted brow. The man went down like a pole-axed steer.

For a long moment Aahz and I considered the fallen man, catching our breath.

" 'Relax, Skeeve! This'll be easy, Skeeve! Trust me, Skeeve.' Boy, Aahz, when you miss a call you don't do it small, do you?"

"Shut up, kid!"

He was rummaging through his pouch again.

"I don't want to shut up, I want to know what happened to the 'foolproof' spell you taught me."

"I was kind of wondering that myself." He had produced the

mirror again and was peering into it. "Tell you what, kid. Check his aura and watch for anything unusual."

" 'Shut up, kid! Check his aura, kid!' You'd think I was some kind of....Hey!"

"What is it?"

"His aura! It's a sort of a reddish yellow except there's a blue patch on his chest."

"I thought so!!" Aahz was across the clearing in a bound, crouching at the fallen man like a beast of prey.

"Look at this!!"

On a thong around the man's neck was a crude silver charm depicting a salamander with one eye in the center of its forehead.

"What is it?"

"I'm not sure, but I've got a hunch. Now play along with me on this. I want you to remove the shape warp spell."

"What spell?"

"C'mon, kid, wake up! The spell that's changing my face."

"That's what I mean. What spell?"

"Now look, kid! Don't give me a lot of back talk. Just do it! He'll be waking up soon."

With a sigh I shut my eyes and set about the seemingly pointless task. It was easier this time, imagining Garkin's face, then melting away the features until Aahz's face was leering at me in my mind's eye. I opened my eyes and looked at Aahz. He looked like Aahz. Terrific.

"Now what?"

As if in answer, the warrior groaned and sat up. He shook his head as if to clear it and opened his eyes. His gaze fell on Aahz, whereupon he blinked, looked again, and reached for his sword, only to find it missing. Also missing were his dagger and hand-axe. Apparently Aahz had not been idle while I was removing the spell.

Aahz spoke first.

"Relax, stranger. Things are not as they seem."

The man sprang to his feet and struck a fighting stance, fists clenched.

"Beware, demon!" he intoned hollowly. "I am not without defenses."

"Oh yeah? Name three. But like I say, relax. First of all, I'm not a demon."

"Know you, demon, that this charm enables me to look through any spells and see you as you really are."

So that was it! My confidence in my powers came back with a rush.

"Friend, though you may not believe me, the sight of that

talisman fills me with joy, for it enables me to prove what I am about to tell you."

"Do not waste your lies on me. Your disguise is penetrated! You are a demon!"

"Right. Could you do me one little favor?" Aahz leisurely sat cross-legged on the ground. "Could you take the charm off for a minute?"

"Take it off?" For a moment the man was puzzled, but he quickly rallied his forces. "Nay, demon. You seek to trick me into removing my charm that you might kill me!"

"Look, dummy. If we wanted to kill you we could have done it while you were knocked out cold!"

For the first time, the man seemed doubtful.

"That is, indeed, a fact."

"Then could you humor me for a moment and take the charm off?"

The warrior hesitated, then slowly removed the charm. He looked hard at Aahz and scowled.

"That's strange. You still look like a demon!"

"Correct, now let me ask you a question. Am I correct in assuming from your words you have some knowledge of demons?"

"I have been a demon hunter for over fifteen years now," he declared proudly.

"Oh, yeah?" For a minute I was afraid Aahz was going to blow the whole gambit, but he got himself back under control and continued.

"Then tell me, friend. In your long experience with demons, have you ever met one who looked like a demon?"

"Of course not! They always use their magik to disguise them."

Fat lot he knew about demons!

"Then that should prove my point!"

"What point?"

I thought for a moment Aahz was going to take him by the shoulders and shake him. It occurred to me that perhaps Aahz's subtleties were lost on this world.

"Let me try, Aahz. Look, sir. What he's trying to say is that if he were a demon he wouldn't look like a demon, but he does so he isn't."

"Oh!" said the man with sudden understanding.

"Now you've lost me," grumbled Aahz.

"But if you aren't a demon, why do you look like one?"

"Ahh...," Aahz sighed, "therein lies the story. You see, I'm accursed!"

"Accursed?"

"Yes. You see, I am a demon hunter like yourself. A rather

successful one, actually. Established quite a name for myself in the field."

"I never heard of you," grumbled the man.

"Well, we've never heard of you either," I chimed in.

"You don't even know my name!"

"Oh, I'm sorry." I remembered my manners. "I'm Skeeve, and this...demon hunter is Aahz."

"Pleased to meet you. I am known as Quigley."

"If I could continue...."

"Sorry, Aahz."

"As I was saying, I had achieved a certain renown among the demons due to my unprecedented success. At times it was rather bothersome, as when it was learned I was coming, most demons would either flee the territory or kill themselves."

"Does he always brag this much?"

"He's just getting started."

"Anyway...one day I was closing with a demon, a particularly ugly brute, when he startled me by addressing me by name. 'Aahz!' says he, 'Before you strike, you should know your career is at an end!' Of course I laughed at him, for I had slain demons more fierce than he, sometimes in pairs. 'Laugh if you will,' he boomed, 'but a conclave of demons empowered me to deal with you. Whether you kill me or not, you are doomed to suffer the same end you have visited on so many of us.' I killed him of course, assuming he was bluffing, but my life has not been the same ever since."

"Why not?"

"Because of the curse! When I returned to my horse, my faithful squire here took one look at me and fainted dead away."

"I did no such thing! I mean...it was the heat."

"Of course, Skeeve." Aahz winked slyly at Quigley.

"At any rate, I soon discovered to my horror that the demon had worked a spell on me before he expired, causing me to take on the appearance of a demon to all who beheld me."

"Fiendish. Clever, but fiendish."

"You see the subtlety of their plan! That I, fiercest of demon hunters, am now hunted in turn by my fellow humans. I am forced to hide like an animal with only my son here for companionship."

"I thought you said he was your squire."

"That, too. Oh, the irony of it all."

"Gee, that's tough. I wish I could do something to help."

"Maybe you can," Aahz smiled winningly.

Quigley recoiled. I found it reassuring that someone else shared my reaction to Aahz's smile.

"Um...how? I mean, I'm just a demon hunter."

"Precisely how you might be of assistance. You see, at the moment we happen to have several demons following us. It occurs to me we might be of mutual service to each other. We can provide you with targets, and you in turn can rid us of a bloody nuisance."

"They're bloody?" Quigley was horrified.

"Just an expression. Well, what do you say? Is it a deal?"

"I dunno. I'm already on a mission and I don't usually take on a new job until the last one's complete. The misinformed might think I was quitting or had been scared off or something. That sort of thing is bad for the reputation."

"It'd be no trouble at all," Aahz persisted. "It's not like you'll have to go out of your way. Just wait right here and they'll be along."

"Why are they following you, anyway?"

"A vile magician sent them after us after I was foolish enough to seek his aid. The curse, you know."

"Of course...wait a minute. Was that magician's name Garkin by any chance?"

"As a matter of fact it was. Why? Do you know him?"

"Why, he's my mission! That's the man I'm going to kill."

"Why?" I interrupted. "Garkin's no demon."

"But he consorts with demons, lad." Aahz scowled warningly at me. "That's enough for any demon hunter. Right, Quigley?"

"Right. Remember that, lad."

I nodded vigorously at him, feeling suddenly very nervous about this whole encounter.

"Where did you hear about Garkin anyway, Quigley?" Aahz asked casually.

"Strangely enough, from an innkeeper...Isstvan, I think he said his name was...a bit strange, but a sincere enough fellow. About three weeks ride back..., but we were talking about your problem. Why did he send demons after you?"

"Well, as I said, I sought him out to try to get him to remove any curse. What I did not realize was that he was actually in league with demons himself. He had heard of me, and flatly refused me aid. What is more, after we left he set some of his demons on our trail."

"I see. How many of them did you say there were?"

"Just two." Aahz assured him. "We've caught glimpses of them occasionally."

"Very well," concluded Quigley. "I'll do it. I'll assist you in your battle."

"That's fine except for one thing. We won't be here."

"Why not? I should think that as a demon hunter you'd welcome the chance once the odds were even."

"If I were here there would be no fight," Aahz stated grandly. "As I have said, I have a certain reputation among demons. If they saw me here they would simply flee."

"I frankly find that hard to believe," commented Quigley.

I was inclined to agree with him, but kept my silence.

"Well, I must admit their fear of my charmed sword has a bit to do with their reluctance to do battle."

"Charmed sword?"

"Yes." Aahz patted the sword at his side. "This weapon once belonged to the famous demon hunter Alfans De Clario."

"Never heard of him."

"Never heard of him? Are you sure you're a demon hunter? Why the man killed over two hundred demons with this sword. They say it is charmed such that whomever wields it cannot be killed by a demon."

"How did he die?"

"Knifed by an exotic dancer. Terrible."

"Yes, they're nasty that way. But about the sword, does it work?"

"It works as well as any sword, a little point-heavy, maybe, but...."

"No. I mean the charm. Does it work?"

"I can testify that I haven't been killed by a demon since I started using it."

"And demons actually recognize it and flee from its owner?"

"Exactly. Of course, I haven't had occasion to use it for years. Been too busy trying to get this curse removed. Sometimes I've thought about selling it, but if I ever get back into business it would be a big help in...um...reestablishing my reputation."

I suddenly realized what Aahz was up to. Quigley rose to the bait like a hungry pike-turtle.

"Hmm...." he said. "Tell you what. Just to give a hand to a fellow demon hunter who's down on his luck, I'll take it off your hands for five gold pieces."

"Five gold pieces! You must be joking. I paid three hundred for it. I couldn't possibly let it go for less than two hundred."

"Oh, well, that counts me out. I only have about fifty gold pieces on me."

"Fifty?"

"Yes, I never travel with more than...."

"But then again, times have been hard, and seeing as how you would be using it to do battle against the fiends who put the curse on me.... Yes, I think I could let you have it for fifty gold pieces."

"But that's all the money I have."

"Yes, but what good is a fat purse if you're torn asunder by a demon?"

"True enough. Let me see it."

He took the blade and hefted, giving it a few experimental swings.

"Crummy balance." He grimaced.

"You get used to it."

"Lousy steel," he declared, squinting at the blade.

"Nice edge on it, though."

"Well, my trainer always told me 'If you take care of your sword, it will take care of you!'"

"We must have had the same trainer."

The two of them smiled at each other. I felt slightly ill.

"Still, I dunno. Fifty pieces of gold is a lot."

"Just look at those stones in the handle."

"I did. They're fake."

"Aha! They're made to look fake. It hides their value."

"Sure did a nice job. What kind of stones are they?"

"Blarney stones."

"Blarney stones?"

"Yes. They're said to ensure your popularity with the ladies, if you know what I mean."

"But fifty gold pieces is all the money I have."

"Tell you what. Make it forty-five gold pieces and throw in your sword."

"My sword?"

"Of course. This beauty will take care of you, and your sword will keep my squire and I from being defenseless in this heathen land."

"Hmm. That seems fair enough. Yes, I believe you have made a deal, my friend."

They shook hands ceremoniously and began effecting the trade. I seized the opportunity to interrupt.

"Gee, it's a shame we have to part so soon."

"Why so soon?" The warrior was puzzled.

"No need to rush off," Aahz assured him, giving me a solid elbow in the ribs.

"But Aahz, we wanted to travel more before sundown and Quigley has to prepare for battle."

"What preparations?" asked Quigley.

"Your unicorn," I continued doggedly. "Don't you want to catch your unicorn?"

"My unicorn! All of my armor is on that animal!"

"Surely it won't wander far...." Aahz growled.

"There are bandits about who would like nothing better than to get their hands on a good war unicorn." Quigley heaved himself to his feet. "And I want him at my side to help me fight the demons. Yes, I must be off. I thank you for your assistance, my friends. Safe journey until we meet again."

With a vague wave of his hand, he disappeared into the woods whistling for his mount.

"Now what was all that about?" Aahz exploded angrily.

"What, Aahz?"

"The big rush to get rid of him. As gullible as he was, I could have traded him out of his pants or anything else vaguely valuable he might have had on him. I specifically wanted to get my hands on that charm."

"Basically I wanted to see him on his way before he caught on to the flaw in your little tale."

"What, the son-nephew slip? He wouldn't have...."

"No, the other thing."

"What other thing?"

I sighed.

"Look, he saw through your disguise because that pendant lets him see through spells, right?"

"Right, and I explained it away saying I was the victim of a demon's curse...."

"...that changed your appearance with a spell. But if he could see through spells, he should be able to see through that spell to see you as a normal man. Right?"

"Hmm....Maybe we'd better be on our way now that we know where Isstvan is."

But I was unwilling to let my little triumph go so easily.

"Tell me, Aahz. What would you do if we encountered a demon hunter as smart as me?"

"That's easy." He smiled, patting the crossbow. "I'd kill him. Think about it."

I did.

Chapter Seven:

"Is there anything in the universe more beautiful and protective than the simple complexity of a spider's web?"

CHARLOTTE

I closed my eyes for concentration. This was more difficult than drawing energies from the force line directly into my body. I pointed a finger for focus, pointing at a spot some five yards distant from me.

The idea of drawing energies from a distant location and controlling them would have seemed impossible to me, until Aahz pointed out it was the same as the candle lighting exercise I had already mastered. Now it did not seem impossible, merely difficult.

Confidently, I narrowed my concentration, and in my mind's eye saw a gleaming blue light appear at the designated point. Without breaking my concentration, I moved my finger overhead in a slow arc. The light followed the lead, etching a glowing blue trail in the air behind it. As it touched the ground again, or where I sensed the ground to be, I moved my finger again, moving the light into the second arc of the protective pentagram.

It occurred to me that what I was doing was not unlike forming the normal flat pentagram Garkin had used at the hut. The only difference being that instead of being inscribed on the floor, this was etched overhead with its points dipping downward to touch the earth. It was more an umbrella than a border.

The other major difference, I thought as I completed the task, was that I was doing it. Me. Skeeve. What I had once watched with awe, I was now performing as routine.

I touched the light down in its original place, completing the pentagram. Quietly pleased, I stood for a moment, eyes closed.

Studying the glowing blue lines etched in my mind's eye.

"Terrific, kid," came Aahz's voice. "Now what say you damp it down a bit before we draw every peasant and demon hunter in the country."

Surprised, I opened my eyes.

The pentagram was still there! Not imagined in my mind, but actually glowing overhead. Its cold blue light gave an eerie illumination to the scene that negated the warmth of our little campfire.

"Sorry, Aahz." I quickly eased my control on the energy and watched as the lines of the pentagram faded to invisibility. They were still there. I could feel their presence in the night air above me. Now, however, they could not be seen by normal vision.

More for the joy of it than out of any lack of confidence, I closed my eyes again and looked at them. They glowed there in shimmering beauty, a cooler, reassuring presence to counter the impatience of the red-gold glow of the force-line spear pointing doggedly toward tomorrow's path.

"Sit down, kid, and finish your lizard-bird."

We were out of the forest proper now, but despite the presence of the nearby road, game was still plentiful and fell ready victim to my snares. Aahz still refused to join me in the meals, insisting alcohol was the only thing in this dimension worth consuming, but I dined frequently and royally.

"You know, kid," he said, looking up from his endless sword-sharpening. "You're really coming along pretty well with your studies."

"What do you mean?" I mumbled through a bone, hoping he would elaborate.

"You're a lot more confident with your magik. You'd better watch your controls, though. You had enough energy in that pentagram to fry anything that bumped against it."

"I guess I'm still a bit worried about the assassins."

"Relax, kid. It's been three days since we set 'em up in that ambush of Quigley's. Even if he didn't stop 'em, they'll never catch up with us now."

"Did I really summon up that much power?" I urged, eager for praise.

"Unless you're actually engaged in magical battle, wards are used as a warning signal only. If you put too much energy into them it can have two potentially bad side effects. First, you can draw unnecessary attention to yourself by jarring or burning an innocent bystander who blunders into it. Second, if it actually reaches a magical opponent, it probably won't stop him; just alert him that he has a potentially dangerous foe in the area."

"I thought it was a good thing if I could summon up lots of power."

"Look, kid. This isn't a game. You're tapping into some very powerful forces here. The idea is to strengthen your control, not see how much you can liberate. If you get too careless with experimenting, you could end up helpless when the actual crunch comes."

"Oh," I said, unconvinced.

"Really, kid. You've got to learn this. Let me try an example. Suppose for a minute you're a soldier assigned to guard a pass. Your superiors put you on the post and give you a stack of ten pound rocks. All you have to do is watch to see if anyone comes, and if they do, drop a rock on their head. Are you with me so far?"

"I guess so."

"Fine. Now it's a long, boring duty, and you have lots of time to think. You're very proud of your muscles, and decide it's a bit insulting that you were only given ten pound rocks. Twenty pound rocks would be more effective, and you think you could handle them as easily as the ten pound variety. Logical?"

I nodded vaguely, still not sure what he was driving at.

"Just to prove the point to yourself, you heft a twenty pound rock, and, sure enough, you can handle it. Then it occurs to you if you can handle a twenty pounder, you should be able to handle a forty pounder, or even a fifty pounder. So you try. Then it happens."

He was getting so worked up I felt no need to respond.

"You drop it on your foot, or you pull a muscle, or you keel over from heat exhaustion, or any one of a hundred other things. Then where are you?"

He leveled an accusing finger at me.

"The enemy strolls through the pass you're supposed to be guarding and you can't even lift the original ten pound rock to stop them. All because you indulged in needless testing of idiotic muscle power!"

I was impressed, and gave the matter serious thought before replying.

"I see what you're saying, Aahz, but there's one flaw in your example. The keyword is 'needless.' Now in my case, it's not a matter of having a stack of ten pound rocks that would do the job. I have a handful of gravel. I'm trying to scrounge around for a rock big enough to do some damage."

"True enough," Aahz retorted, "but the fact remains if you overextend yourself you won't be able to use what you already have. Even gravel can be effective if used at the right time. Don't underrate what you've got or what you're doing. Right now you're keeping the finder spear going, maintaining the wards, and keeping my disguise intact. That's a lot for someone of your abilities to be doing simultaneously. If something happened right now, which would you drop first?"

"Um...."

"Too late! We're already dead. You won't have time to ponder energy problems. That's why you always have to hold some back to deal with immediate situations while you rally your energies from other activities. Now do you see?"

"I think so, Aahz," I said haltingly. "I'm a bit tired."

"Well, think about it. It's important. In the meantime get some sleep and try to store up your energies. Incidentally, let the finder spear go for now. You can summon it up again in the morning. Right now, it's just a needless drain."

"Okay, Aahz. How about your disguise?"

"Hmm...better keep that. It'll be good practice for you to maintain both that and the wards in your sleep. Speaking of which...."

"Right, Aahz."

I drew my acquired assassin's cloak about me for warmth and curled up. Despite his gruff manner, Aahz was persistent that I get enough sleep as well as food.

Sleep did not come easily, however. I found I was still a bit wound up over casting the wards.

"Aahz?"

"Yeah, kid?"

"How would you say my powers right now stack up against the devils?"

"What devils?"

"The assassins that were following us."

"I keep telling you, kid. Those weren't Deveels, those were Imps."

"What's the difference?"

"I told you before. Imps are from Imper, and Deveels...."

"...are from Deva," I finished for him. "But what does that mean? I mean, are their powers different or something?"

"You'd better believe it, kid." Aahz snorted. "Deveels are some of the meanest characters you'd ever not want to tangle with. They're some of the most feared and respected characters in the dimensions."

"Are they warriors? Mercenaries?"

Aahz shook his head.

"Worse!" he answered. "They're merchants."

46

"Merchants?"

"Don't sneer, kid. Maybe merchants is too sedate a phrase to describe them. Traders Supreme is more like it."

"Tell me more, Aahz."

"Well, history was never my forte, but as near as I can tell, at one time the entire dimension Deva faced economic ruin. The lands suffered a plague that affected the elements. Fish could not live in its oceans, plants could not grow in the soil. Those plants that did grow were twisted and changed and poisoned the animals. The dimension was no longer able to support the life of its citizenry."

I lay, staring up at the stars as Aahz continued his tale.

Dimension travel, once a frivolous pastime, now became the key to survival. Many left Deva, migrating singly or in groups to other dimensions. Their tales of their barren, miserable homeland served as a prototype for many religious groups' concept of an afterworld for evil souls.

"The ones who stayed, however, decided to use the power of dimension travel in a different way. They established themselves as traders, traveling the dimensions buying and selling wonders. What is common in one dimension is frequently rare in another. As the practice grew, they became rich and powerful...also the shrewdest hagglers in all the dimensions. Their techniques for driving a hard bargain have been passed down from generation to generation and polished until now they are without equal. They are scattered through the dimensions, returning to Deva only occasionally to visit the Bazaar."

"The Bazaar?" I prompted.

"No one can travel extensively in all the dimensions in one lifetime. The Bazaar on Deva is the place the Deveels meet to trade with each other. An off-dimension visitor there will be sore pressed to not lose o'er much, much less hold his own. It's said if you make a deal with a Deveel, you'd be wise to count your fingers afterward...then your arms and legs, then your relatives...."

"I get the picture. Now how about the Imps?"

"The Imps." Aahz said the word as if it tasted bad. "The Imps are inferior to the Deveels in every way."

"How so?"

"They're cheap imitations. Their dimension, Imper, lies close to Deva, and the Deveels bargain with them so often they're almost bankrupt from the irresistible 'fair deals.' To hold their own, they've taken to aping the Deveels, attempting to peddle wonders through the dimensions. To the uneducated, they may seem clever and powerful; in fact, occasionally they try to pass themselves off as Deveels. Compared to the masters, however, they're bungling incompetents."

He trailed off into silence. I pondered his words, and they prompted another question.

"Say, Aahz?"

"Hmm? Yeah, kid?"

"What dimension do you come from?"

"Perv."

"Does that make you a Pervert?"

"No. That makes me a Pervect. Now shut up!"

I assumed he wanted me to go to sleep, and maintained silence for several minutes. There was just one more question I had to ask, however, if I was going to get any sleep at all.

"Aahz?"

"Keep it down, kid."

"What dimension is this?"

"Hmmm? This is Klah, kid. Now for the last time, shut up."

"What does that make me, Aahz?"

There was no answer.

"Aahz?"

I rolled over to look at him. He was staring out into the darkness and listening intently.

"What is it?"

"I think we've got company, kid."

As if in response to his words, I felt a tremor in the wards as something came through.

I bounded to my feet as two figures appeared at the edge of the firelight. The light was dimming, but was sufficient to reveal the fact that both figures were wearing the hooded cloaks of assassins, and the gold side was out!

Chapter Eight:

"In times of crisis, it is of utmost importance not to lose one's head."

M. ANTOINETTE

The four of us stood in frozen tableau for several minutes studying each other. My mind was racing, but could not focus on the definite course of action. I decided to follow Aahz's lead and simply stood regarding the two figures cooly, trying to ignore the two crossbows leveled steadily on us.

Finally, one of our visitors broke the silence.

"Well, Throckwoddle? Aren't you going to invite your friends to sit down?"

Surprisingly, this was addressed to me!

"Ummm...." I said.

"Yes, Throckwoddle," Aahz drawled, turning to me. "And aren't you going to introduce me to your colleagues?"

"Um...." I repeated.

"Perhaps he doesn't remember us," the second figure injected sarcastically.

"Nonsense," responded the first with equal sarcasm. "His two oldest friends? Brockhurst and Higgens? How could he possibly not remember our names? Just because he forgot to share the loot doesn't mean he'd forget our names. Be fair, Higgens."

"Frankly, Brockhurst," responded the other. "I'd rather he remembered the loot and forgot our names."

Their words were stuffy and casual, but the crossbows never wavered.

I was beginning to get the picture. Apparently these were the two Imps Aahz had assured me couldn't overtake us. Fortunately, it seemed they thought I was the Imp who had killed Garkin...at least I thought it was fortunate.

"Gentlemen," Aahz exclaimed, stepping forward. "Let me say what a great pleasure it is to...."

He stopped as Brockhurst's crossbow lept to his shoulder in one smooth move.

"I'm not sure who you are," he intoned. "But I'd advise you to stay out of this. This is a private matter between the three of us."

"Brockhurst," interrupted Higgens. "It occurs to me we may be being a bit hasty in our actions."

"Thank you, Higgens," I said, greatly relieved.

"Now that we've established contact," he continued, favoring me with an icy glare, "I feel we should perhaps secure our traveling companion before we continue this...discussion."

"I suppose you're right, Higgens," Brockhurst admitted grudgingly. "Be a good fellow and fetch him along while I watch these two."

"I feel that would be ill-advised on two counts. First, I refuse to approach that beast alone, and second, that would leave you alone facing two to one odds, if you get my point."

"Quite. Well, what do you suggest?"

"That we both fetch our traveling companion and return without delay."

"And what is to keep these two from making a hasty departure?"

"The fact that we'll be watching them from somewhere in the darkness with crossbows. I believe that should be sufficient to discourage them from making...ah...any movements which might be subject to misinterpretation."

"Very well," Brockhurst yielded grudgingly. "Throckwoddle, I would strongly suggest you not attempt to avoid us further. While I don't believe we could be any more upset with you than we already are, that might actually succeed in provoking us further."

With that, the two figures faded back into darkness.

"What are we going to do, Aahz?" I whispered frantically.

He seemed not to hear me.

"Imps!" he chortled, rubbing his hands together gleefully. "What a stroke of luck!"

"Aahz! They're going to kill me!"

"Hm? Relax, kid. Like I said, Imps are gullible. If they were really thinking, they would have shot us down without talking. I haven't met an Imp yet I couldn't talk circles around."

He cocked his head, listening.

"They're coming back now. Just follow my lead. Oh yes...I almost forgot. Drop the disguise on my features when I give you the cue."

"But you said they couldn't catch...."

I broke off as the two Imps reappeared. They were leading a war unicorn between them. The hoods of the cloaks were back now, revealing their features. I was moderately surprised to see they looked human, seedy perhaps, but human nonetheless. Then I saw Quigley.

He was sitting woodenly astride the unicorn, lurching back and forth with the beast's stride. His eyes were staring fixedly straight ahead and his right arm was raised as if in salutation. The light of the fire reflected off his face as if it were glass, and I realized with horror he was no longer alive, but a statue of some unidentified substance.

Any confidence I might have gained from Aahz's assurances left me in a rush. Gullible or not, the Imps played for keeps, and any mistake we made would in all likelihood be our last.

"Who's that?" Aahz asked, interrupting my thoughts.

I realized I had been dangerously close to showing a betraying sign of recognition of the statue.

"There will be time for that later, if indeed there is a later," said Higgens, grimly dropping the unicorn's reins and raising his crossbow.

"Yes," echoed Brockhurst, imitating Higgen's move with his own weapon. "First there is a matter of an explanation to be settled. Throckwoddle?"

"Gentlemen, Gentlemen," said Aahz soothingly, stepping between me and the crossbows. "Before you proceed I must insist on introducing myself properly. If you will but allow me a moment while I remove my disguise."

The sight of the two weapons had rattled me so badly I almost missed my cue. Fortunately, I managed to gather my scattered senses and closed my eyes, shakily executing the change features spell to convert Aahz back to his normal dubious appearance.

I'm not sure what reaction I had expected from the Imps at the transformation, but the one I got surpassed any possible expectations.

"By the Gods below!" gasped Brockhurst.

"A Pervert!" gasped Higgens.

"That's Pervect!" smiled Aahz, showing all his pointed teeth. "And don't ever forget it, friend Imps."

"Yessir!" they chorused in unison.

They were both standing in slack-jawed amazement, crossbows dangling forgotten in their hands. From their terrified reactions, I began to suspect that despite all his bragging, Aahz had perhaps not told me everything about his dimension or the reputation of its inhabitants.

Aahz ignored their stares and plopped down again at his place by the fire.

"Now that that's established, why don't you put away those silly crossbows and sit down so we can chat like civilized folk, eh?"

He gestured impatiently and they hastened to comply. I also resumed a sitting position, not wishing to be the only one left standing.

"But...what are...why are you here...sir...if you don't mind my asking?" Brockhurst finally managed to get the whole question out.

However incompetent he might be as a demon, he sure knew how to grovel.

"Ah!" smiled Aahz. "Therein lies the story."

I settled back. This could take a while.

"I was summoned across the dimensions barrier by one Garkin, a magician I have never cared much for. It seems he was expecting some trouble from a rival and was eager to enlist my aid for the upcoming fracas. Now, as I said before, I had never been fond of Garkin and was not particularly wild about joining him. He began growing unpleasant in his insistence to the point that I considered swaying from my normal easy going nature to take action against him, when who should appear but Throckwoddle here who did me the favor of putting a quarrel into the old slime-stirrer."

Aahz acknowledged me with an airy wave. I tried to look modest.

"Naturally we fell to chatting afterward, and he mentioned he was in the employment of one Isstvan and that his action against Garkin had been part of an assignment."

"You answered questions about an assignment?" Higgens turned to me aghast.

"Yes I did," I snarled at him. "Wouldn't you, considering the circumstances?"

"Oh, yes...of course...." He darted a nervous glance at Aahz and lapsed into respectful silence again.

"Anyway," Aahz continued, "it occurred to me I owed this fellow Isstvan a favor for ridding me of a nagging nuisance, so I suggested I accompany Throckwoddle back to his employer that I might offer him my services, on a limited basis, of course."

"You could have waited for us." Brockhurst glowered at me.

"Well...I wanted...you see...I...."

"I insisted," Aahz smiled. "You see, my time is quite valuable and I had no desire to waste it waiting around."

"Oh," said Brockhurst.

Higgens was not so easily swayed.

"You could have left us a message," he muttered.

"We did," Aahz replied. "My ring, in full view on the table. I see you found it."

He pointed an accusing finger at Brockhurst. I noticed for the first time the Imp was wearing Garkin's ring.

"This ring?" Brockhurst started. "Is it yours? I thought it was part of Garkin's loot that had been overlooked."

"Yes, it's mine." Aahz bared his teeth. "I'm surprised you didn't recognize it. But now that we're united, you will, of course, return it."

"Certainly!" the Imp fumbled in his haste to remove the ring.

"Careful there," Aahz cautioned. "You do know how to operate it, don't you? It can be dangerous in ignorant hands."

"Of course I know how to operate it," Brockhurst replied in an injured tone. "You press against the ring with the fingers on either side of it. I saw one like it at the Bazaar on Deva once."

He tossed the ring to Aahz who caught it neatly and slipped it on his finger. Fortunately it fit. I made a mental note to ask Aahz to let me try using the ring sometime, now that we knew how it worked.

"Now that I've explained about me, how about answering my question," Aahz said, leveling a finger at the Quigley statue. "Who is that?"

"We aren't sure ourselves," Higgens admitted.

"It's all quite puzzling, really," Brockhurst added.

"Would you care to elaborate on that?" Aahz prompted.

"Well, it happened about three days back. We were following your trail to...um...with hopes of reuniting our group. Suddenly this warrior gallops out of the brush ahead of us and bars our path. It was as if he knew we were coming and was waiting for us. 'Isstvan was right!' he shouts, 'This region *does* abound with demons!' "

"Isstvan?" I said, doing my best to look puzzled.

"That's what he said. It surprised us, too. I mean, here we are working for Isstvan, and were set upon by a man claiming to be sent by the same employer. Anyway, then he says, 'Behold the weapon of your doom!' and draws a sword."

"What kind of sword was it?" Aahz asked innocently.

"Nothing special. Actually a little substandard from all we could see. Well, it put us in a predicament. We had to defend ourselves, but were afraid to harm him on the off-chance he really was working for Isstvan."

"What did you do?" I asked.

"Frankly, we said 'to heck with it' and took the easy way out. Higgens' here bounced one of his stone balls off the guy's forehead and froze him in place. We've been dragging him along ever since. We figure we'll dump him in Isstvan's lap and let him sort it out."

"A wise solution," commented Aahz.

They inclined their heads graciously at the compliment.

"One question I'd like to ask," I interjected. "How were you able to overtake us, encumbered as you were?"

"Well, it was no small problem. We had little hope of overtaking you as it was, and with our new burden, it appeared it would be impossible," Brockhurst began.

"We were naturally quite eager to...ah...join you, so we resorted to desperate measures," Higgens continued. "We took a side trip to Twixt and sought the aid of the Deveel there. It cost us a pretty penny, but he finally agreed to teleport our group to the trail ahead of you, allowing us to make our desired contact."

"Deveel? What Deveel?" Aahz interrupted.

"Frumple. The Deveel at Twixt. The one who...."

Brockhurst broke off suddenly, his eyes narrowing suspiciously. He shot a dark glance at Higgens, who was casually reaching for his crossbow.

"I'm surprised Throckwoddle hasn't mentioned Frumple to you," Higgens purred. "After all, he's the one who told us about him."

Chapter Nine:

"To function efficiently, any group of people or employees must have faith in their leader."

CAPT. BLIGH (ret.)

"Yes, Throckwoddle." If anything, Aahz's voice was even more menacing than the Imps. "Why didn't you tell me about the Deveel?"

"It...ah...must have slipped my mind," I mumbled.

With a massive exertion of self control, I shot my most withering glare at the Imps, forcing myself to ignore the menace of the crossbows. I was rewarded by seeing them actually look guilty and avoid my gaze.

"Slipped your mind! More likely you were trying to hold back a bit of information from me," Aahz said accusingly. "Well, now that it's out, let's have the rest of it. What about this Deveel?"

"Ask Brockhurst," I grumbled. "He seems to be eager to talk about it."

"Well, Brockhurst?" Aahz turned to him.

The Imp gave me an apologetic shrug as he started.

"Well, I guess I've already told you most of it. There's a Deveel, Frumple, in residence in Twixt. He goes under the cover of Ahbul the Rug Merchant, but he actually maintains a thriving trade in the usual Deva manner, buying and selling across the dimensions."

"What's he doing in Klah?" Aahz interrupted. "I mean there's not much business here. Isn't it a little slow for a Deveel's taste?"

"Well, Throckwoddle said...." Brockhurst broke off and shot me a look.

"Go on, tell him." I tried to sound resigned.

"Well," the Imp continued, "rumor has it that he was exiled from

Deva and is in hiding here, ashamed to show his face in a major dimension."

"Barred from Deva? Why? What did he do?"

I was glad Aahz asked. It would have sounded strange coming from me.

"Throckwoddle wouldn't tell us. Said Frumple was sensitive on the subject and we shouldn't bring it up."

"Well, Throckwoddle?" Aahz turned to me.

I was so caught up in the story it took me a few beats before I remembered that I really didn't know.

"Um...I can't tell you." I said.

"What?" Aahz scowled.

I began to wonder how much he was caught up in the story and had lost track of the realities of the situation.

"I learned his secret by accident and hold it as a personal confidence," I said haughtily. "During our travels these last few days, I've learned some rather interesting items about you and hold them in the same esteem. I trust you will respect my silence on the matter of Frumple as I expect others to respect my silence about those matters pertaining to you."

"Okay, okay. You've made your point." Aahz conceded.

"Say...um...Throckwoddle," Higgens interrupted. "I would suggest we all shed our disguises like our friend Perver...um, Pervect here has. No sense in using up our energies keeping up false faces among friends."

His tone was casual, but he sounded suspicious. I noticed he had not taken his hand off his crossbow.

"Why?" argued Brockhurst. "I prefer to keep my disguise on at all times when in another dimension. Lessens the chance of forgetting to put it on at a crucial moment."

"I think Higgens is right," Aahz stated before I could support Brockhurst. "I for one like to see the true faces of the people I'm talking to."

"Well," grumbled Brockhurst, "if everyone is going to insist."

He closed his eyes in concentration, and his features began to shimmer and melt.

I didn't watch the whole process. My mind was racing desperately back to Garkin's hut, when Aahz held up the charred face of the assassin. I hastily envisioned my own face next to it and began working, making certain obvious modifications to its appearance to repair the fire damage.

When I was done, I snuck a peek out of one eye. The other two had changed already. My attention was immediately drawn to their complexion. Theirs was a pinkish red, while mine wasn't. I hastily re-closed my eye and made the adjustment.

Satisfied now, I opened my eyes and looked about me. The other two Imps now showed the apparently characteristic pointed ears and chins. Aahz looked like Aahz. The situation had completely reversed since the Imps had arrived. Instead of being normal surrounded by three disguised demons, I was now surrounded by three demons while I was disguised. Terrific.

"Ahh. That's better," chortled Aahz.

"You know, Throckwoddle," Higgens said, cocking a head at me. For a moment there in the firelight you looked different. In fact...."

"Come, come, gentlemen," Aahz interrupted. "We have serious matters to discuss. Does Isstvan know about Frumple's existence?"

"I don't believe so," answered Brockhurst. "If he did, he would have either enlisted him or had him assassinated."

"Good," exclaimed Aahz. "He could very well be the key to our plot."

"What plot?" I asked.

"Our plot against Isstvan, of course."

"What?" exclaimed Higgens, completely distracted from me now. "Are you insane?"

"No," retorted Aahz. "But Isstvan is. I mean, think! Has he been acting particularly stable?"

"No," admitted Brockhurst. "But then neither has any other magician I've met, present company included."

"Besides," Higgens interrupted, "I thought you were on your way to help him."

"That's before I heard your story," Aahz pointed out. "I'm not particularly eager to work for a magician who pits his own employees against each other."

"When did he do that?" Higgens asked.

Aahz made an exasperated gesture.

"Think, gentlemen! Have you forgotten our stony-faced friend there?" He jerked a thumb at the figure on the unicorn. "If you recall your tale correctly, his words seemed to imply he had been sent by Isstvan to intercept you."

"That's right," said Brockhurst. "So?"

"What do you mean, 'So?' " Aahz exploded. "That's it! Isstvan sent him to kill you. Either he was trying to cut his overhead by assassinating his assassins before payday, or he's so unstable mentally he's lashing out blindly at everyone, including his own allies. Either way he doesn't sound like the most benevolent of employers."

"You know, I believe he has a point there," I observed, determined to be of some assistance in this deception.

"But if that's true, what are we to do?" asked Higgens.

"Well, I don't have a firm plan of action," Aahz admitted. "But I have some general ideas that might help."

"Such as?" prompted Brockhurst.

"You go back to Isstvan. Say nothing at all of your suspicions. If you do, he might consider you dangerous and move against you immediately. What's more, refuse any new assignments. Find some pretext to stay as close to him as possible. Learn all about his habits and weaknesses, but don't do anything until we get there."

"Where are you going?" asked Higgens.

"We are going to have a little chat with Frumple. If we're going to move against Isstvan, the support of a Deveel could be invaluable."

"And probably unobtainable," grumpled Brockhurst. "I've never known a Deveel yet to take sides in a fight. They prefer being in a position to sell to both sides."

"What do you mean 'we?' " asked Higgens. "Isn't Throckwoddle coming with us?"

"No. I've developed a fondness for his company. Besides, if he doesn't agree to help us, it would come in handy to have an assassin close by. Frumple's too powerful to run the risk of leaving him unallied to help Isstvan."

As Aahz was speaking, Brockhurst casually leaned back out of his line of vision and silently mouthed the word "Pervert" at Higgens. Higgens quietly nodded his agreement, and they both shot me sympathetic glances.

"Well, what do you think?" Aahz asked in conclusion.

"Hmm...what do we do with him?" Higgins indicated the Quigley statue with a jerk of his head.

"We'll take him with us," I chimed in hastily.

"Of course!" agreed Aahz, shooting me a black look. "If you two took him back to Isstvan, he might guess you suspected his treachery."

"Besides," I added, "maybe we can revive him and convince him to join us in our battle."

"I suppose you'll be wanting the antidote then." Higgins sighed, fishing a small vial from inside his cloak and tossing it to me. "Just sprinkle a little on him and he'll return to normal in a few minutes. Watch yourself, though. There's something strange about him. He seemed to be able to see right through our disguises."

"Where's the sword you were talking about?" Aahz asked.

"It's in his pack. Believe me, it's junk. The only reason we brought it along was that he seemed to put so much stock in it. It'll be curious to find out what he thought it was when we revive him."

Well, I believe that just about covers everything," Brockhurst sighed. "I suggest we get some sleep and start on our respective journeys first thing in the morning."

"I suggest you start on your journey now," Aahz said pointedly.

"Now?" Brockhurst exclaimed.

"But it's the middle of the night," Higgens pointed out.

"Might I remind you gentlemen that the longer you are away from Isstvan, the greater the chances are he'll send another assassin after you."

"He's right, you know," I said thoughtfully.

"I suppose so," grumbled Higgens.

"Well," said Brockhurst, rising to his feet,"I guess we'll be on our way then as soon as we divide Garkin's loot."

"On the contrary," stated Aahz. "Not only do we not divide the loot, I would suggest you give us whatever funds you have at your disposal."

"What?" they chorused, their crossbows instantly in their hands again.

"Think, gentlemen," Aahz said soothingly. "We'd be trying to bargain with a Deveel for his support. As you yourselves have pointed out, they are notoriously unreasonable in their prices. I would hate to think we might fail in our negotiations for a lack of funds."

There was a pregnant silence as the Imps sought to find a hole in his logic.

"Oh, very well," Brockhurst conceded at last, lowering his crossbow and reaching for his purse.

"I still don't think it will do any good," Higgens grumbled, imitating Brockhurst's move. "You probably couldn't buy off a Deveel if you had the Gnomes themselves backing you."

They passed the purses over to Aahz, who hefted them judiciously before tucking them into his own waistband.

"Trust me, gentlemen." Aahz smiled. "We Pervects have methods of persuasion that are effective even on Deveels."

The Imps shuddered at this and began edging away.

"Well...umm...I guess we'll see you later," Higgens mumbled. "Watch yourself, Throckwoddle."

"Yes," added Brockhurst. "And be sure when you're done, the Deveel is either with us or dead."

I tried to think of something to say in return, but before anything occurred to me they were gone.

Aahz cocked an eyebrow at me and I held up a restraining hand until I felt them pass through the wards. I signaled him with a nod.

"They've gone," I said.

"Beautiful!" exclaimed Aahz gleefully. "Didn't I tell you they were gullible?"

For once I had to admit he was right.

"Well, get some sleep now, kid. Like I said before, tomorrow's going to be a busy day, and all of a sudden it looks like it's going to be even busier."

I complied, but one question kept nagging at me.

"Aahz?"

"Yeah, kid."

"What dimension do the Gnomes come from?"

"Zoorik," he answered.

On that note, I went to sleep.

Chapter Ten:

"Man shall never reach his full capacity while chained to the earth. We must take wing and conquer the heavens."

ICARUS

"Are you sure we're up to handling a Deveel, Aahz?" I was aware I had asked the question countless times in the last few days, but I still needed reassurance.

"Will you relax, kid?" Aahz growled. "I was right about the Imps, wasn't I?"

"I suppose so," I admitted hesitantly.

I didn't want to tell Aahz, but I wasn't that happy with the Imp incident. It had been a little too close for my peace of mind. Since the meeting, I had been having reoccurring nightmares involving Imps and crossbows.

"Look at it this way, kid. With any luck this Frumple character will be able to restore my powers. That'd take you off the hotseat."

"I guess so," I said without enthusiasm.

He had raised this point several times since learning about Frumple. Each time he did, it gave me the same feeling of discomfort.

"Something bothering you, kid?" Aahz asked, cocking his head at me.

"Well...it's...Aahz, if you do get your powers back, will you still want me as an apprentice?"

"Is that what's been eating at you?" he seemed genuinely surprised. "Of course I'll still want you. What kind of a magician do you think I am? I don't choose my apprentices lightly."

"You wouldn't feel I was a burden?"

"Maybe at first, but not now. You were in at the start of this

Isstvan thing, you've earned the right to be in on the end of it."

Truth to tell, I wasn't all that eager to be there when Aahz confronted Isstvan, but that seemed to be the price I would have to pay if I was going to continue my association with Aahz.

"Um...Aahz?"

"Yeah, kid?"

"Just one more question?"

"Promise?"

"How's that?"

"Nothing. What's the question, kid."

"If you get your powers back, and I'm still your apprentice, which dimension will we live in?"

"Hmm. To be honest, kid, I hadn't really given it much thought. Tell ya what, we'll burn that bridge when we come to it, okay?"

"Okay, Aahz."

I tried to get my mind off the question. Maybe Aahz was right. No sense worrying about the problem until we knew for sure it existed. Maybe he wouldn't get his powers back. Maybe I'd get to be the one to fight Isstvan after all. Terrific.

"Hey! Watch the beast, kid!"

Aahz's voice broke my train of thought. We were leading the war unicorn between us, and the beast chose this moment to act up.

It nickered and half-reared, then planted its feet and tossed its head.

"Steady...ow!"

Aahz extended a hand trying to seize its bridle and received a solid rap on the forearm from the unicorn's horn for his trouble.

"Easy, Buttercup," I said soothingly. "There's a good boy."

The beast responded to my coaxings, first by settling down, pawing the ground nervously, then finally by rubbing his muzzle against me.

Though definitely a friendly gesture, this is not the safest thing to have a unicorn do to you. I ducked nimbly under his swinging horn and cast about me quickly. Snatching an orange flower from a nearby bush, I fed it to him at an arm's length. He accepted the offering and began to munch it contentedly.

"I don't think that beast likes demons," Aahz grumbled sullenly. rubbing his bruised arm.

"It stands to reason," I retorted. "I mean, he *was* a demon hunter's mount, you know."

"Seems to take readily enough to you, though," Aahz observed. "Are you sure you're not a virgin?"

"Certainly not," I replied in my most injured tones.

Actually I was, but I would have rather been fed to vampire-slugs than admit it to Aahz.

"Speaking of demon hunters, you'd better check on our friend there," Aahz suggested. "It could get a bit grisly if an arm or something broke off before we got around to restoring him."

I hastened to comply. We had rigged a drag litter for the Quigley-statue to avoid having to load and unload him each night, not to mention escaping the chore of saddling and unsaddling the war unicorn. The bulk of the gear and armor was sharing the drag-litter with the Quigley-statue, a fact which seemed to make the unicorn immensely happy. Apparently it was far easier to drag all that weight than to carry it on one's back.

"He seems to be okay, Aahz," I reported.

"Good," he sneered. "I'd hate to think of anything happening to him, accidental-like."

Aahz was still not happy with our traveling companions. He had only grudgingly given in to my logic for bringing them along as opposed to leaving them behind. I had argued that they could be of potential assistance in dealing with the Deveel, or at least when we had our final show-down with Isstvan.

In actuality, that wasn't my reasoning at all. I felt a bit guilty about having set Quigley up to get clobbered by the Imps and didn't want to see any harm befall him because of it.

"It would make traveling a lot easier if we restored him," I suggested hopefully.

"Forget it, kid."

"But Aahz...."

"I said forget it! In case you've forgotten, that particular gentleman's major pastime seems to consist of seeking out and killing demons. Now I'm aware my winning personality may have duped you into overlooking the fact, but I am a demon. As such, I am not about to accept a living, breathing, and most importantly, functioning demon hunter as a traveling companion."

"We fooled him before!" I argued.

"Not on a permanent basis. Besides, when would you practice your magik if he was restored? Until we meet with the Deveel, you're still our best bet against Isstvan."

I wished he would stop mentioning that. It made me incredibly uncomfortable when he did. Besides, I couldn't think of a good argument to it.

"I guess you're right, Aahz," I admitted.

"You'd better believe I'm right. Incidentally, since we seem to be stopped anyway, this is as good a time as any for your next lesson."

My spirits lifted. Besides my natural eagerness to extend my magical abilities, Aahz's offer contained an implied statement that he was pleased with my progress so far in earlier lessons.

"Okay, Aahz," I said, looping the unicorn's reins around a nearby bush. "I'm ready."

"Good," smiled Aahz, rubbing his hands together. "Today we're going to teach you to fly."

My spirits fell again.

"Fly?" I asked.

"That's what I said, kid. Fly. Exciting, isn't it?"

"Why?"

"Whadya mean, why? Ever since we first cast jealous eyes on the creatures of the air we've wanted to fly. Now you're getting a chance to learn. That's why it's exciting!"

"I meant, why should I want to learn to fly?"

"Well...because everybody wants to fly."

"I don't," I said emphatically.

"Why not?"

"I'm afraid of heights, for one thing," I answered.

"That isn't enough reason to not learn," Aahz scowled.

"Well, I haven't heard any reasons yet as to why I should." I scowled back at him.

"Look, kid," Aahz began coaxingly, "It isn't so much flying as floating on air."

"The distinction escapes me," I said dryly.

"Okay, kid. Let me put it to you this way. You're my apprentice, right?"

"Right," I agreed suspiciously.

"Well, I'm not going to have an apprentice that can't fly! Get me!?" he roared.

"All right, Aahz. How does it work?" I knew when I was beaten.

"That's better. Actually it doesn't involve anything you don't already know. You know how to levitate objects, right?"

I nodded slowly, puzzled.

"Well, all flying is is levitating yourself."

"How's that again?"

"Instead of standing firm on the ground and lifting an object, you push against the ground with your will and lift yourself."

"But if I'm not touching the ground, where do I draw my power from?"

"From the air! C'mon, kid, you're a magician, not an elemental."

"What's an elemental?"

"Forget it. What I meant was you aren't bound to any of the four elements, you're a magician. You control them, or at least influence them and draw your power from them. When you're flying, all you have to do is draw your power from the air instead of the ground."

"If you say so, Aahz," I said doubtfully.

"Okay, first locate a force line."

"But we left it when we started off to see the Deveel," I argued.

"Kid, there are lots of force lines. Just because we left one of the ground force lines doesn't mean we're completely out of touch. Check for a force line in the air."

"In the air?"

"Believe me, kid. Check."

I sighed and closed my eyes. Turning my face skyward, I tried to picture the two-headed spear. At first I couldn't do it, then realized with a start I was seeing a spear, but a different spear. It wasn't as bright as the last spear had been, but glowed softly with icy blues and whites.

"I think I've got one, Aahz!" I gasped.

"It's blue and white, right?" Aahz sneered sarcastically.

"Yes, but it's not as bright as the last one."

"It's probably further away. Oh well, it's close enough for you to draw energy from. Well, give it a try, kid. Hook into that force line and push the ground away. Slowly now."

I did as I was instructed, reaching out with my mind to tap the energies of that icy vision. The surge of power I felt was unlike any I had experienced before. Whereas before when I summoned the power I felt warm and swollen with power, this time I felt cool and relaxed. The power flow actually made me feel lighter.

"Push away, kid," came Aahz's voice. "Gently!"

Lazily I touched the ground with my mind, only casually aware of the curious sensation of not physically feeling anything with my feet.

"Open your eyes, kid! Adjust your trim."

Aahz's voice came to me from a strange location this time. Surprised, my eyes popped open.

I was floating some ten feet above the ground at an angle that was rapidly drifting toward a horizontal position. I was flying!

The ground came at me in a rush. I had one moment of dazed puzzlement before it slammed into me with jarring reality.

I lay there for a moment forcing air back into my lungs and wondering if I had broken anything.

"Are you okay, kid?" Aahz was suddenly looming over me. "What happened anyway?"

"I...I was flying!" I forced the words at last.

"Yeah, So? Oh, I get it. You were so surprised you forgot to maintain the energy flow, right?"

I nodded, unable to speak.

"Of all the dumb...look, kid, when I tell you you're going to fly, believe it!"

"But...."

"Don't 'but' me! Either you believe in me as a teacher or you don't! There's no buts about it!"

"I'm sorry, Aahz." I was getting my breath back again.

"Ahh...didn't mean to jump on you like that, kid, but you half scared me to death with that fall. You've got to understand we're starting to get into some pretty powerful magik now. You've got to expect them to work. A surprise-break like that last one with the wrong thing could get you killed, or me for that matter."

"I'll try to remember, Aahz. Shall I try it again?"

"Just take it easy for a few minutes, kid. Flying can take a lot out of you, even without the fall."

I closed my eyes and waited for my head to stop whirling.

"Aahz?" I said finally.

"Yeah, kid?"

"Tell me about Perv."

"What about it?"

"It just occurred to me, those Imps seemed scared to death when they realized you were a Pervect. What kind of a reputation does your dimension have?"

"Well," he began, "Perv is a self-sufficient, stand-offish dimension. We may not have the best fighters, but they're close enough that other dimension travelers give them lots of room. Technology and magik exist side by side and are intertwined with each other. All in all it makes a pretty powerful little package."

"But why should anyone be afraid of that?"

"As I said, Perv has a lot going for it. One of the side effects of success is an abundance of hangers-on. There was a time when we were close to being swamped with refugees and immigrants from other dimensions. When they got to be too much of a nuisance, we put a stop to it."

"How?" I pushed.

"First, we took the non-contributing outsiders and ran 'em out. Then, for an added measure of insurance, we encouraged the circulation of rumors of certain anti-social attitudes of Pervects toward those from other dimensions."

"What kind of rumors?"

"Oh, the usual. That we eat our enemies, torture folks for amusement and have sexual practices that are considered dubious by any dimension's standards. Folks aren't sure how much is truth and how much is exaggeration, but they're none to eager to find out first hand."

"How much of it is true, Aahz?" I asked propping myself up on

one elbow.

He grinned evilly at me.

"Enough to keep 'em honest."

I was going to ask what it took to be considered a contributing immigrant, but decided to let it pass for a while.

Chapter Eleven:

"One of the joys of travel is visiting new towns and meeting new people."

G. KHAN

"Ah! What a shining example of civilization!" chortled Aahz exuberantly as he peered about him, delighted as a child on his first outing.

We were sauntering casually down one of the lesser used streets of Twixt. Garbage and beggars were strewn casually about while beady rodent eyes, human and inhuman, studied us from the darkened doors and windows. It was a cluster of buildings crouched around an army outpost which was manned more from habit than necessity. The soldiers we occasionally encountered had degenerated enough from the crisp, recruiting poster model that it was frequently difficult to tell which seemed more menacing and unsavory, the guards or the obviously criminal types they were watching.

"If you ask me, it looks more like mankind at its worst!" I mumbled darkly.

"That's what I said, a shining example of civilization!"

There wasn't much I could say to that, not feeling like getting baited into another one of Aahz's philosophical lectures.

"Aahz, is it my imagination or are people staring at us?"

"Relax, kid. In a town like this the citizens will always instinctively size up a stranger. They're trying to guess if we're victims or victimizer. Our job is to make sure they think we're in the second category."

To illustrate his point he suddenly whirled and crouched like a cat, glaring back down the street with a hand on his sword hilt.

There was sudden movement at the windows and doorways as roughly a dozen half-seen forms melted back into the darkness.

One figure didn't move. A trollop leaning on a window-sill, her arms folded to display her ill-covered breasts, smiled invitingly at him. He smiled and waved. She ran an insolent tongue tip slowly around her lip and winked broadly.

"Um...Aahz?"

"Yeah, kid?" he replied, without taking his eyes from the girl.

"I hate to interrupt, but you're supposed to be a doddering old man, remember?"

Aahz was still disguised as Garkin, a fact which seemed to have momentarily slipped his mind.

"Hmm? Oh, yeah. I guess you're right, kid. It doesn't seem to bother anybody else though. Maybe they're used to feisty old men in this town."

"Well, could you at least stop going for your sword? That's supposed to be our surprise weapon."

Aahz was wearing the assassin's cloak now, which he quickly pulled forward again to hide his sword.

"Will you get off my back, kid? Like I said, nobody seems to be paying any attention."

"Nobody?" I jerked my head pointedly toward the girl in the window.

"Her? She's not paying any more attention to us than she is anyone else on the street."

"Really?"

"Well, if she is, it's more because of you than because of me."

"Me? C'mon, Aahz."

"Don't forget, kid, you're a pretty impressive person now."

I blinked. That hadn't occurred to me. I had forgotten I was disguised as Quigley now.

We had hidden the demon hunter just outside of town...well, actually we buried him. I had been shocked by the suggestion at first, but as Aahz pointed out, the statue didn't need any air and it was the only surefire way we had of ensuring he wouldn't be found by anyone else.

Even the war unicorn following us, now fully saddled and armored, did not help me keep my new identity in mind. We had been traveling together too long now.

I suppose I should have gotten some satisfaction from the fact I could now maintain not only one, but two disguises without consciously thinking about it. I didn't. I found it unnerving that I had to remember other people were seeing me differently than I was seeing myself.

I shot a glance as the trollop. As our eyes met, her smile broadened noticeably. She displayed her increased enthusiasm by leaning further out of the window until I began to worry about her falling out...of the window or her dress.

"What did I tell you, kid!" Aahz slapped me enthusiastically on the shoulder and winked lewdly.

"I'd rather she was attracted to me for me as I really am," I grumbled darkly.

"The price of success, kid," Aahz responded philosophically. "Well, no matter. We're here on business, remember?"

"Right," I said firmly.

I turned to continue our progress, and succeeded only in whacking Aahz soundly in the leg with my sword.

"Hey! Watch it, kid!"

It seemed there was more to this sword-carrying than met the casual eye.

"Sorry, Aahz," I apologized. "This thing's a bit point-heavy."

"Yeah? How would you know?" my comrade retorted.

"Well...you said...."

"I said? That won't do it, kid. What's point-heavy for me may not be point heavy for you. Weapon balance is a personal thing."

"Well...I guess I'm just not used to wearing a sword," I admitted.

"It's easy. Just forget you're wearing it. Think of it as part of you."

"I did. That's when I hit you."

"Hmm...we'll go into it more later."

Out of the corner of my eye, I could still see the trollop. She clapped her hands in silent applause and blew me a kiss. I suddenly realized she thought I had deliberately hit Aahz, a premeditated act to quell a rival. What's more, she approved of the gesture.

I looked at her again, more closely this time. Maybe later I would give Aahz the slip for a while and....

"We've got to find Frumple." Aahz's voice interrupted my wandering thoughts.

"Hmm...? Oh. How, Aahz?"

"Through quick and cunning. Watch this, kid."

So saying, he shot a quick glance up and down the street. A pack of three urchins had just rounded the corner, busily engaged in a game of keep-away with one of the group's hat.

"Hey!" Aahz hailed them. "Where can I find the shop of Abdul the Rug Dealer?"

"Two streets up and five to the left," they called back, pointing the direction.

"See, kid? That wasn't hard."

"Terrific," I responded, unimpressed.

"Now what's wrong, kid?"

"I thought we were trying to avoid unnecessary attention."

"Don't worry, kid."

"Don't worry!? We're on our way to meet a Deveel on a supposedly secret mission, and you seem to be determined to make sure everybody we see notices us and knows where we're going."

"Look, kid, how does a person normally act when they come into a new town?"

"I don't know," I admitted. "I haven't been in that many towns."

"Well, let me sketch it out for you. They want to be noticed. They carry on and make lots of noise. They stare at the women and wave at people they've never seen before."

"But that's what we've been doing."

"Right! Now do you understand?"

"No."

Aahz heaved an exasperated sigh.

"C'mon, kid. Think a minute, even if it hurts. We're acting like anyone else would walking into a strange town, so nobody will look at us twice. They won't pay any more attention to us than they would any other newcomer. Now if we followed your suggestion and came skulking into town, not talking to anyone or looking at anything, and tried real hard not to be noticed, then everyone and his kid brother would zero in on us trying to figure out what we were up to. Now do you understand?"

"I...I think so."

"Good...cause there's our target."

I blinked and looked in the direction of his pointing finger. There squatting between a blacksmith's forge and a leather-worker's displays was the shop. As I said, I was new to city life, but I would have recognized it as a rug merchant's shop even if it was not adorned with a large sign proclaiming it such. The entire front of the shop was lavishly decorated with colorful geometric patterns apparently meant to emulate the patterns of the rugs inside. I guess it was intended to look rich and prosperous. I found it unforgivably gaudy.

I had been so engrossed in our conversation, I had momentarily forgotten our mission. With the shop now confronting us at close range, however, my nervousness came back in a rush.

"What are we going to do, Aahz?"

"Well, first of all I think I'm going to get a drink."

"A drink?"

"Right. If you think I'm going to match wits with a Deveel on an empty stomach, you've got another think coming."

"A drink?" I repeated, but Aahz was gone, striding purposefully toward a nearby tavern. There was little for me to do but follow, leading the unicorn.

The tavern was a dingy affair, even to my rustic eye. A faded awning sullenly provided shade for a small cluster of scarred wooden tables. Flies buzzed around a cat sleeping on one of the tables...at least I like to assume it was asleep.

As I tied the unicorn to one of the awning supports, I could hear Aahz bellowing at the innkeep for two of his largest flagons of wine. I sighed, beginning to despair that Aahz would never fully adapt to his old-man disguise. The innkeep did not seem to notice any irregularity between Aahz's appearance and his drinking habits, however. It occurred to me that Aahz might be right in his theories of how to go unnoticed. City people seemed to be accustomed to loud rude individuals of any age.

"Sit down, kid," Aahz commanded. "You're making me nervous hovering around like that."

"I thought we were going to talk with the Deveel," I grumbled, sinking into a chair.

"Relax, kid. A few minutes one way or the other won't make that much difference. Besides, look!"

A young, well-dressed couple was entering the rug shop.

"See? We couldn't have done any business anyway. At least not until they left. The kind of talk we're going to have can't be done in front of witnesses. Ahh!"

The innkeeper had arrived, clinking the two flagons of wine down on the table in a lack-luster manner.

"About time!" Aahz commented seizing a flagon in each hand and immediately draining one. "Aren't you going to have anything, kid?"

A toss of his head and the second flagon was gone.

"While my friend here makes up his mind, bring me two more...and make them decent sizes this time if you have to use a bucket!"

The innkeep retreated, visibly shaken. I wasn't. I had already witnessed Aahz's capacity for alcohol, astounding in an era noted for heavy drinkers. What did vex me a bit was that the man had departed without taking my order.

I did eventually get my flagon of wine, only to find my stomach was too nervous to readily accept it. As a result, I wound up sipping it slowly. Not so Aahz. He continued to belt them down at an alarming rate. For quite some time he drank. In fact, we sat for nearly an hour, and there was still no sign of the couple who had entered the shop.

Finally, even Aahz began to grow impatient.

"I wonder what's taking them so long," he grumbled.

"Maybe they're having trouble making up their mind," I suggested.

"C'mon, kid. The shop's not that big. He can't have too large a selection."

He downed the last of his wine and stood up.

"We've waited long enough," he declared. "Let's get this show on the road."

"But what about the couple?" I reminded him.

"We'll just have to inspire them to conclude their business with a bit more speed."

That had a vaguely ominous ring to it, and Aahz's toothy grin was additional evidence that something unpleasant was about to happen.

I was about to try to dissuade him, but he started across the street with a purposeful stride that left me standing alone.

I hurried to catch up with him, leaving the unicorn behind in my haste. Even so, I was unable to overtake him before he had entered the shop.

I plunged after him, fearing the worst. I needn't have worried. Except for the proprietor, the shop was empty. There was no sign of the couple anywhere.

Chapter Twelve:

"First impressions are of major importance in business matters."

J. PIERPONT FINCH

"May I help you, gentlemen?"

The proprietor's rich robes did not successfully hide his thinness. I am not particularly muscular. . .as Skeeve, that is. . .but I had the impression that if I struck this man, he wouldn't bruise, he'd shatter. I mean, I've seen skinny men before, but he seemed to be a skeleton with a too-small skin stretched over the bones.

"We'd like to talk with Abdul," Aahz said loftily.

"I am he, and he is I," recited the proprietor. "You see before you Abdul, a mere shadow of a man, pushed to the brink of starvation by his clever customers."

"You seem to be doing all right for yourself," I murmured, looking about me.

The shop was well stocked, and even my untraveled eye could readily detect the undeniable signs of wealth about. The rugs were delicately woven in soft fabrics unfamiliar to me, and gold and silver shone from the depths of their designs. Obviously these rugs were intended for the wealthy, and it seemed doubtful their current owner would be suffering from a lack of comfort.

"Ahh. Therein lies the tale of my foolishness," cried the proprietor wringing his hands. "In my blind confidence, I sank my entire holdings into my inventory. As a result, I starve in the midst of plenty. My customers know this and rob me in my vulnerable times. I lose money on every sale, but a man must eat."

"Actually," Aahz interrupted, "we're looking for something in a deep shag wall-to-wall carpet."

"What's that?...I mean, do not confuse poor Abdul so, my humble business...."

"Come off it, Abdul...or should I say Frumple." Aahz grinned his widest grin. "We know who you are and what you are. We're here to do a little business."

At his words, the proprietor moved with a swiftness I would not have suspected him capable of. He was at the door in a bound, throwing a bolt and lowering a curtain which seemed to be of a substance even more strange than that of his rugs.

"Where'd you learn your manners!" he snarled back over his shoulder in a voice quite unlike the one used by the whiney proprietor. "I've got to live in this town, you know."

"Sorry," Aahz said, but he didn't sound at all apologetic.

"Well, watch it next time you come barging in and start throwing my name around. People here are not particularly tolerant of strange beings or happenings."

He seemed to be merely grumbling to himself, so I seized the opportunity to whisper to Aahz.

"Psst. Aahz. What's a wall-to-wall...."

"Later, kid."

"You!" The proprietor seemed to see me for the first time. "You're the statue! I didn't recognize you moving."

"Well...I...."

"I should have known," he raved on. "Deal with Imps and you invite trouble. Next thing you know every...."

He broke off suddenly and eyed us suspiciously. His hand disappeared into the folds and emerged with a clear crystal. He held it up and looked through it like an eye glass, scrutinizing us each in turn.

"I should have known," he spat. "Would you be so kind as to remove your disguises? I like to know who I'm doing business with."

I glanced at Aahz who nodded in agreement.

Closing my eyes, I began to effect the change to our normal appearance. I had enough time to wonder if Frumple would wonder about my transformation, if he realized I was actually a different person than the statue he had seen earlier. I needn't have worried.

"A Pervert!" Frumple managed to make the word sound slimey.

"That's Pervect if you want to do business with us," Aahz corrected.

"It's Pervert until I see the color of your money," Frumple sneered back.

I was suddenly aware he was studying me carefully.

"Say, you wouldn't by any chance be an Imp named

Throckwoddle, would you?"

"Me? No! I...I'm...."

But he was already squinting at me through the crystal again.

"Hmph," he grunted, tucking his viewer back in his robe. "I guess you're okay. I'd love to get my hands on that Throckwoddle, though. He's been awfully free spreading my name around lately."

"Say, Frumple," Aahz interjected. "You aren't the only one who likes to see who he's doing business with, you know."

"Hm? Oh! Very well, if you insist."

I expected him to close his eyes and go to work, but instead he dipped a hand into his robe again. This time he produced what looked like a small hand mirror with some sort of a dial on the back. Peering into the mirror, he began to gently turn the dial with his fingers.

The result was immediate and startling. Not merely his face, but his whole body began to change, filling out, and taking on a definite reddish hue. As I watched, his brows thickened and grew closer together, his beard line crept us his face as if it were alive, and his eyes narrowed cruelly. Almost as an afterthought, I noted that his feet were now shiny cloven hooves and the tip of a pointed tail appeared at the bottom hem of his robe.

In an impressively short period of time, he had transformed into a...well, a devil!

Despite all my preparations, I felt the prickle of superstitious fear as he put away the mirror and turned to us again.

"Are you happy now?" he grumbled at Aahz.

"It's a start," Aahz conceded.

"Enough banter," Frumple was suddenly animated again. "What brings a Pervert to Klah? Slumming? And where does the kid fit in?"

"He's my apprentice," Aahz informed him.

"Really?" Frumple swept me with a sympathetic gaze. "Are things really that tough, kid? Maybe we could work something out."

"He's quite happy with the situation," interrupted Aahz. "Now let's get to our problem."

"You want me to cure the kid's insanity?"

"Huh? No. C'mon, Frumple. We came here on business. Let's declare a truce for a while, okay?"

"If you insist. It'll seem strange, though; Perverts and Deveels have never really gotten along."

"That's Pervects!"

"See what I mean?"

"Aahz!" I interrupted. "Could you just tell him?"

"Hmm? Oh. Right, kid. Look, Frumple. We've got a problem we

were hoping you could help us with. You see, I've lost my powers."

"What!?" exploded Frumple. "You came here without the magical ability to protect yourself against being followed? That tears it. I spend seven years building a comfortable front here, and some idiot comes along and...."

"Look, Frumple. We told you the kid here's my apprentice. He knows more than enough to cover us."

"A half-trained apprentice! He's trusting my life and security to a half-trained apprentice!"

"You seem to be overlooking the fact we're already here. If anything was going to happen it would have happened already."

"Every minute you two are here you're threatening my existence."

"...which is all the more reason for you to deal with our problem immediately and stop this pointless breast-beating!"

The two of them glared at each other for a few moments, while I tried to be very quiet and unnoticeable. Frumple did not seem to be the right choice for someone to pin our hopes on.

"Oh, all right!" Frumple grumbled at last. "Since I probably won't be rid of you any other way."

He strode to the wall and produced what looked like a length of rope from behind one of the rugs.

"That's more like it," Aahz said triumphantly.

"Sid down and shut up," ordered our host.

Aahz did as he was bid, and Frumple proceeded to circle him. As he moved, the Deveel held the rope first this way, then that, sometimes looped in a circle, other times hanging limp. All the while he stared intently at the ceiling as if reading a message written there in fine print.

I didn't have the faintest idea what he was doing, but it was strangely enjoyable to watch someone order Aahz about and get away with it.

"Hmm...." the Deveel said at last. "Yes, I think we can say that your powers are definitely gone."

"Terrific!" Aahz growled. "Look, Frumple. We didn't come all this way to be told something we already knew. You Deveels are supposed to be able to do anything. Well, do something!"

"It's not that easy, Pervert!" Frumple snapped back. "I need information. How did you lose your powers, anyway?"

"I don't know for sure," Aahz admitted. "I was summoned to Klah by a magician, and when I arrived they were gone."

"A magician? Which one?"

"Garkin."

"Garkin? He's a mean one to cross. Why don't you just get him to restore your powers instead of getting me involved?"

"Because he's dead. Is that reason enough for you?"

"Hmm...that makes it difficult."

"Are you saying you can't do anything?" Aahz sneered. "I should have known. I always thought the reputation of the Deveels was overrated.

"Look, Pervert! Do you want my help or not? I didn't say I couldn't do anything, just that it would be difficult."

"That's more like it," Aahz chortled. "Let's get started."

"Not so fast," interrupted Frumple. "I didn't say I would help you, just that I could."

"I see," sneered Aahz. "Here it comes, kid. The price tag. I told you they were shake-down artists."

"Actually," the Deveel said dryly, "I was thinking of the time factor. It would take a while for me to make my preparations, and I believe I've made my feelings quite clear about you staying here longer than is absolutely necessary."

"In that case," smiled Aahz, "I suggest you get started. I believe I've made *my* feelings quite clear that we intend to stay here until the cure is affected."

"In that case," the Deveel smiled back at him, "I believe *you* raised the matter of cost. How much do you have with you?"

"Well, we have...." I began.

"*That* strikes me as being unimportant," Aahz glared warningly at me. "Suppose you tell us how much you feel is a fair price for your services."

Frumple graced him with one withering glare before sinking thoughtfully into his calculations.

"Hmm...material cost is up...and of course, there's my time...and you did call without an appointment...let's say it would cost you, just as a rough estimate, mind you, oh, in the neighborhood of...Say!"

He suddenly brightened and smiled at us.

"Maybe you'd be willing to work this as a trade. I cure you, and you do me a little favor."

"What kind of a favor?" Aahz asked suspiciously.

For once I was in complete agreement with him. Something in Frumple's voice did not inspire confidence.

"A small thing, really," the Deveel purred. "Sort of a decoy mission."

"We'd rather pay cash," I asserted firmly.

"Shut up, kid," Aahz advised. "What kind of a decoy mission, Frumple?"

"You may have noticed the young couple who entered my shop

ahead of you. You did! Good. Then you have doubtless noticed they are not on the premises currently."

"How did they leave?" I asked curiously.

"I'll get to that in a moment," Frumple smiled. "Anyway, theirs is an interesting if common story. I'll spare you the details, but in re young lovers kept apart by their families. In their desperation, they turned to me for assistance. I obliged them by sending them to another dimension where they can be happy free of their respective family's intervention."

"For a fee, of course," Aahz commented dryly.

"Of course," Frumple smiled.

"C'mon, Aahz," I chided. "It sounds like a decent thing to do, even if he was paid for it."

"Quite so!" beamed the Deveel. "You're quite perceptive for one so young. Anyway, my generosity has left me in a rather precarious position. As you have no doubt noticed, I am quite concerned with my image in this town. There is a chance that image may be threatened if the couple's relatives succeed in tracking them to my shop and no farther."

"That must have been some fee," Aahz mumbled.

"Now my proposition is this: in exchange for my assistance, I would ask that you two disguise yourselves as that couple and lay a false trail away from my shop."

"How much of a false trail?" I asked.

"Oh, it needn't be anything elaborate. Just be seen leaving town by enough townspeople to ensure that attention will be drawn away from my shop. Once out of sight of town, you can change to any disguise you like and return here. By that time, my preparations for your cure should be complete. Well, what do you say? Is it a deal?"

Chapter Thirteen:

"The secret to winning the support of large groups of people is positive thinking."

N. BONAPARTE

"People are staring at us, Aahz."

"Relax, kid. They're supposed to be staring at us."

To illustrate his point, he nodded and waved to a knot of glowering locals. They didn't wave back.

"I don't see why I have to be the girl," I grumbled.

"We went through that before, kid. You walk more like a girl than I do."

"That's what you and Frumple decided. I don't think I walk like a girl at all!"

"Well, let's say I walk less like a girl than you do."

It was hard to argue with logic like that, so I changed subjects.

"Couldn't we at least travel by less populated streets?" I asked.

"Why?" countered Aahz.

"Well, I'm not too wild about having a lot of people seeing me when I'm masquerading as a girl."

"C'mon, kid. The whole idea is that no one would recognize you. Besides, you don't know anybody in this town. Why should you care what they think of you?"

"I just don't like it, that's all," I grumbled.

"Not good enough," Aahz asserted firmly. "Being seen is part of our deal with Frumple. If you had any objections you should have said so before we closed the negotiations."

"I never got a chance," I pointed out. "But since the subject's come up, I do have a few questions."

"Such as?"

"Such as what are we doing?"

"Weren't you paying attention, kid? We're laying a false trail for...."

"I know that," I interrupted. "What I mean is, why are we doing what we're doing? Why are we doing Frumple a favor instead of just paying his price?"

"You wouldn't ask that if you'd ever dealt with a Deveel before," Aahz snorted. "Their prices are sky-high, especially in a case like ours when they know the customer is desperate. Just be thankful we got such a good deal."

"That's what I mean, Aahz. Are we *sure* we've gotten a good deal?"

"What do you mean?"

"Well, from what I've been told, if you think you've gotten a good deal from a Deveel, it usually means you've overlooked something."

"Of course you speak from a wide range of experience," Aahz sneered sarcastically. "Who told you so much about dealing with Deveels?"

"You did," I said pointedly.

"Hmmm. You're right, kid. Maybe I have been a little hasty."

Normally I would have been ecstatic over having Aahz admit I was right. Somehow, however, in the current situation, it only made me feel that much more uncomfortable.

"So what are we going to do?" I asked.

"Well, normally I deal honestly unless I think I'm being double-crossed. This time, however, you've raised sufficient doubt in my mind that I think we should bend the rules a little."

"Situational ethics again?"

"Right!"

"So what do we do?"

"Start looking for a relatively private place where we can dump these disguises without being noticed."

I began scanning the streets and alleys ahead of us. My uneasiness was growing into panic, and it lent intensity to my search.

"I wish we had our weapons along," I muttered.

"Listen to him," Aahz jeered. "It wasn't that long ago you were telling me all about how magicians don't need weapons. C'mon, kid. What would you do with a weapon if you had one?"

"If you want to get specific," I said dryly, "I was wishing *you* had a weapon."

"Oh! Good point. Say...ah...kid? Are you still looking for a private place?"

"Yeah, I've got a couple possibles spotted."

"Well forget it. Start looking for something wide open with a lot of exits."

"Why the change in strategy," I asked.

"Take a look over your shoulder...casual like."

I did as I was bid, though it was not as casual as it might have been. It turned out my acting ability was the least of our worries.

There was a crowd of people following us. They glared at us darkly and muttered to themselves. I wanted very badly to believe we were not the focus of their attention, but it was obvious that was not the case. They were clearly following us, and gathering members as they went.

"We're being followed, Aahz!" I whispered.

"Hey, kid. I pointed them out to you, remember?"

"But why are they following us? What do they want?"

"Well, I don't know for sure, of course, but I'd guess it has something to do with our disguises."

I snuck another glance at the crowd. The interest in us did not seem to be lessening at all. If anything, the crowd was even bigger and looked even angrier. Terrific.

"Say, Aahz?" I whispered.

"Yeah, kid?"

"If they're after us because of our disguises, why don't we just change back?"

"Bad plan, kid. I'd rather run the risk of them having some kind of grudge against the people we're impersonating then facing up to the consequences if they found out we were magicians."

"So what do we do?"

"We keep walking and hope we run into a patrol of soldiers that can offer us some protection."

A fist-sized rock thudded into the street ahead of us, presumably thrown by one of the people following us.

"...or...." Aahz revised hastily, "we can stop right now and find out what this is all about."

"We could run," I suggested hopefully, but Aahz was already acting on his earlier suggestion.

He stopped abruptly and spun on his heel to face the crowd.

"What is the meaning of this?" he roared at the advancing multitude.

The crowd lurched to a halt before the direct address, those in the rear colliding with those in front who had already stopped. They seemed a bit taken aback by Aahz's action and milled about without direction.

I was pleasantly surprised at the success of my companion's maneuver, but Aahz was never one to leave well enough alone.

"Well?" he demanded, advancing on them. "I'm waiting for an explanation."

For a moment the crowd gave ground before his approach. Then an angry voice rang out from somewhere in the back.

"We want to know about our money!"

That opened the door.

"Yeah! What about our money?!"

The cry was taken up by several other voices, and the crowd began to growl and move forward again.

Aahz stood his ground and held up a hand commanding silence.

"What about your money?" he demanded haughtily.

"Oh, no, you don't," came a particularly menacing voice. "You aren't going to talk your way out of it this time!"

A massive bald man brandishing a butcher's cleaver shouldered his way through the crowd to confront Aahz.

"My good man," Aahz sniffed. "If you're implying...."

"I'm implying nothing!" The man growled. "I'm saying it flat out. You and that trollop of yours are crooks!"

"Now, aren't you being just a bit hasty in...."

"Hasty!" the man bellowed. "Hasty! Mister, we've already been too patient with you. We should have run you out of town when you first showed up with your phoney anti-demon charms. That's right, I said phoney! Some of us knew it from the start. Anyone with a little education knows there's no such things as demons."

For a moment I was tempted to let Aahz's disguise drop. Then I looked at the crowd again and decided against it. It wasn't a group to joke with.

"Now, some folks bought the charms because they were gullible, some as a gag, some of us because...well, because everyone else was buying them. But we all bought them, just like we bought your story that they had to be individually made and you needed the money in advance."

"That was all explained at the time," Aahz protested.

"Sure it was. You're great at explanations. You explained it just like you explained away those two times we caught you trying to leave town."

"Well...we...uh," Aahz began.

"Actually," I interrupted, "we were only...."

"Well, we've had enough of your explanations. That's what we told you three days ago when we gave you two days to either come up with the charms or give us our money back."

"But these things take time...."

"You've used up that excuse. Your time was up yesterday. Now do we get our money, or...."

"Certainly, certainly," Aahz raised his hands soothingly.

"Just give me a moment to speak with my colleague."

He smiled at the crowd as he took me by the arm and drew me away.

"What are we going to do, Aahz?"

"*Now* we run," he said calmly.

"Huh?" I asked intelligently.

I was talking to thin air. Aahz was already legging it speedily down the street.

I may be slow at times, but I'm not *that* slow. In a flash I was hot on his heels.

Unfortunately, the crowd figured out what Aahz was up to about the same time I did. With a howl they were after us.

Surprisingly, I overtook Aahz. Either he was holding back so I could catch up, or I was more scared than I thought, which is impossible.

"Now what?" I panted.

"Shut up and keep running, kid," Aahz barked, ducking around a knot of people.

"They're gaining on us," I pointed out.

Actually, the group we had just passed had joined the pursuit, but it had the same effect as if the crowd was gaining.

"Will you knock it off and help me look?" Aahz growled.

"Sure. What are we looking for?"

"A couple dressed roughly like us," he replied.

"What do we do if we see them?"

"Simple," Aahz replied." We plow into them full tilt, you swap our features for theirs, and we let the mob tear *them* apart."

"That doesn't sound right somehow," I said doubtfully.

"Kid, remember what I told you about situational ethics?"

"Yeah."

"Well, this is one of those situations."

I was convinced, though not so much by Aahz's logic as by the rock that narrowly missed my head. I don't know how the crowd managed to keep its speed and still pick up things to throw, but it did.

I began watching for a couple dressed like us. It's harder than it sounds when you're at a dead run with a mob at your heels.

Unfortunately, there was no one in sight who came close to fitting the bill. Whomever it was we were impersonating seemed to be fairly unique in their dress.

"I wish I had a weapon with me," Aahz complained.

"We've already gone through that," I called back. "And besides, what would you do if you had one? The only thing we've got that might stop them is the fire ring."

"Hey! I'd forgotten about that," Aahz gasped. "I've still got it on."

"So what?" I asked. "We can't use it."

"Oh, yeah? Why not?"

"Because then they'd know we're magicians."

"That won't make any difference if they're dead."

Situational ethics or not, my stomach turned at the thought of killing that many people.

"Wait, Aahz!" I shouted.

"Watch this, kid." He grinned and pointed his hand at them.

Nothing happened.

Chapter Fourteen:

"A little help at the right time is better than a lot of help at the wrong time."

TEVYE

"C'mon, Aahz!" I shouted desperately, overturning a fruit stand in the path of the crowd.

Now that it seemed my fellow-humans were safe from Aahz, my concern returned to making sure he was safe from them.

"I don't believe it!" Aahz shouted, as he darted past.

"What?" I called, sprinting after him.

"In one day I believed both a Deveel and an Imp. Tell you what, kid. If we get out of this, I give you my permission to kick me hard. Right in the rump, twice."

"It's a deal!" I panted.

This running was starting to tax my stamina. Unfortunately, the crowd didn't seem tired at all. That was enough to keep me running.

"Look, kid!" Aahz was pointing excitedly. "We're saved."

I followed his finger. A uniformed patrol was marching...well, sauntering down the street ahead of us.

"It's about time," I grumbled, but I was relieved nonetheless.

The crowd saw the soldiers, too. Their cries increased in volume as they redoubled their efforts to reach us.

"C'mon, kid! Step on it!" Aahz called. "We're not safe yet."

"Step on what?" I asked, passing him.

Our approach to the patrol was noisy enough that by the time we got there, the soldiers had all stopped moving and were watching the chase. One of them, a bit less unkempt than the others, had shouldered his way to the front of the group and stood sneering at us with folded arms. From his manners, I guessed he was an officer. There was no other explanation for the others allowing him to act the way he was.

I skidded to a stop in front of him.

"We're being chased!" I panted.

"Really?" he smiled.

"Let me handle this, kid," Aahz mumbled, brushing me aside. "Are you the officer in charge, sir?"

"I am," the man replied.

"Well, it seems that these...citizens," he pointed disdainfully at our pursuers, "intend us bodily harm. A blatant disregard for your authority...sir!"

The mob was some ten feet distant and stood glaring alternately at us and the soldiers. I was gratified to observe that at least some of them were breathing hard.

"I suppose you're right," the officer yawned. "We should take a hand in this."

"Watch this, kid," Aahz whispered, nudging me in the ribs as the officer stepped forward to address the crowd.

"All right. You all know it is against the law for citizens to inflict injuries on each other," he began.

The crowd began to grumble darkly, but the officer waved them into silence as he continued.

"I know, I know. We don't like it either. If it were up to us we'd let you settle your own differences and spend our time drinking. But it's not up to us. We have to follow the laws the same way you do, and the laws say only the military can judge and punish the citizenry."

"See?" I whispered. "There are some advantages to civilization."

"Shut up, kid," Aahz hissed back.

"So even though I know you'd love to beat these two to a bloody pulp, we can't let you do it. They must be hanged in accordance with the law!"

"What?"

I'm not sure if I said it, or Aahz, or if we cried out in unison. Whichever it was, it was nearly drowned out in the enthusiastic roar of the crowd.

A soldier seized my wrists and twisted them painfully behind my back. Looking about, I saw the same thing had happened to Aahz. Needless to say, this was not the support we had been hoping for.

"What did you expect?" the officer sneered at us. "If you wanted help from the military, you shouldn't have included us on your list of customers. If we had had our way, we would have strung you up a week ago. The only reason we held back was these yokels had given you extra time and we were afraid of a riot if we tried anything."

Our wrists were secured by thongs now. We were slowly being herded toward a lone tree in front of one of the open air restaurants.

"Has anyone got some rope?" the officer called to the crowd.

Just our luck, somebody did. It was passed rapidly to the officer, who began ceremoniously tying nooses.

"Psst! kid!" Aahz whispered.

"What now?" I mumbled bitterly.

My faith in Aahz's advice was at an all time low.

"When they go to hang you, fly!"

"What?"

Despite myself, I was seized with new hope.

"C'mon, kid. Wake up! Fly. Like I taught you on the trail."

"They'd just shoot me down."

"Not fly away, dummy. Just fly. Hover at the end of the rope and twitch. They'll think you're hanging."

I thought about it...hard. It might work, but...I noticed they were tossing the nooses over a lower limb of the tree.

"Aahz! I can't do it. I can't levitate us both. I'm not that good yet."

"Not both of us, kid. Just you. Don't worry about me."

"But...Aahz...."

"Keep my disguise up, though. If they figure out I'm a demon they'll burn the bodies...both of them."

"But Aahz...."

We were out of time. Rough hands shoved us forward and started fitting the nooses over our heads.

I realized with a start I had no time to think about Aahz. I'd need all my concentration to save myself, if there was even time for that!

I closed my eyes and sought desperately for a force line in the air. There was one there...faint, but there. I began to focus on it.

The noose tightened around my neck and I felt my feet leave the ground. I felt panic rising in me and forced it down.

Actually it was better this way. They should feel weight on the rope as they raised me. I concentrated on the force line again...focus ...draw the energies...redirect them.

I felt a slight loosening of the noose. Remembering Aahz's lectures on control, I held the energies right there and tried an experimental breath. I could get air! Not much, it was true, but enough to survive.

What else did I have to do? Oh yes, I had to twitch. I thought back to how a squirrel-badger acted when caught in a snare.

I kicked my legs slightly and tried an experimental tremor. It had the overall effect of tightening the noose. I decided to try another tactic. I let my head loll to one side and extended my tongue out of the corner of my mouth.

It worked. There was a sudden increase in the volume of the catcalls from the crowd to reward my efforts.

I held that pose.

My tongue was rapidly drying out, but I forced my mind away from it. To avoid involuntarily swallowing, I tried to think of other things.

Poor Aahz. For all his gruff criticism and claims of not caring for anyone else but himself, his last act had been to think of my welfare. I promised myself that when I got down from here....

What would happen when I got down from here? What do they do with bodies in this town? Do they bury them? It occurred to me it might be better to hang than be buried alive.

"The law says they're supposed to hang there until they rot!"

The officer's voice seemed to answer my thoughts and brought my mind back to the present.

"Well, they aren't hanging in front of the law's restaurant!" came an angry voice in response.

"Tell you what. We'll come back at sundown and cut them down."

"Sundown? Do you realize how much money I could lose before sundown? Nobody wants to eat at a place where a corpse dangles it's toes in his soup. I've already lost most of the lunch rush!"

"Hmm...It occurs to me that if the day's business means that much to you, you should be willing to share a little of the profit."

"So that's the way it is, is it? Oh, very well. Here...for your troubles."

There was the sound of coins being counted out.

"That isn't very much. I have to share with my men, you know."

"You drive a hard bargain! I didn't know bandits had officers."

More coins were counted, accompanied by the officer's chuckle. It occurred to me that instead of studying magik, I should be devoting my time to bribes and graft. It seemed to work better.

"Men!" the officer called. "Cut this carrion down and haul it out of town. Leave it at the city limits as a warning to anyone else who would seek to cheat the citizens of Twixt."

"You're too considerate." The restaurant owner's voice was edged with sarcasm.

"Think nothing of it, citizen," the officer sneered.

I barely remembered to stop flying before they cut the rope. I bit my tongue as I started into the ground, and risked sneaking it back into my mouth. No one noticed.

Unseen hands grabbed me under the armpits and by the ankles, and the journey began to the city limits.

Now that I knew I wasn't going to be buried, my thoughts returned to my future.

First, I would have to do something to Frumple. What, I wasn't sure, but something. I owed Aahz that much. Maybe I could restore Quigley and enlist his aid. He was supposed to be a demon hunter. He was probably better equipped to handle a Deveel than I was. Then again, remembering Quigley, that might not be a valid assumption.

Then there was Isstvan. What was I going to do about him? I wasn't sure I could beat him with Aahz's help. Without it, I wouldn't stand a chance.

"This should be far enough. Shall we hang them again?"

I froze at the suggestion. Fortunately the voice at my feet had different ideas.

"Why bother? I haven't seen an officer yet who'd move a hundred paces from a bar. Let's just dump 'em here."

There was a general chorus of assent, and the next minute I was flying through the air again. I tried to relax for the impact, but the ground knocked the wind out of me again.

If I was going to continue my efforts to master flying, I'd have to devote more time to the art of forced landings.

I lay there motionless. I couldn't hear the soldiers any more, but I didn't want to run the risk of sitting up and betraying the fact I wasn't dead.

"Are you going to lay there all day or are you going to help me get untied?"

My eyes flew open involuntarily. Aahz was sitting there grinning down at me.

There was only one sensible thing to do, and I did it. I fainted.

Chapter Fifteen:

*"Anyone who uses the phrase 'easy as taking candy
from a baby' has never tried taking candy from a
baby."*

R. HOOD

"Can we move now?" I asked.

"Not yet, kid. Wait until the lights have been out for a full day."

"You mean a full hour."

"Whatever. Now shut up and keep watching."

We were waiting in the dead-end alley across the street from Frumple's shop. Even though we were supposedly secure in our new disguises, I was uneasy being back in the same town where I had been hung. It's a hard feeling to describe to someone who hasn't experienced it. Then too, it was strange being with Aahz after I had gotten used to the idea of him being dead.

Apparently the neck muscles of a Pervect are considerably stronger than those of a human. Aahz had simply tensed those muscles and they provided sufficient support to keep the noose from cutting off his air supply.

As a point of information, Aahz had further informed me that his scales provided better armor than most chain-mail or plate armor available in this dimension. I had heard once that demons could only be destroyed by specially constructed weapons or by burning. It seemed the old legends may have actually had some root in fact.

"Okay, kid," Aahz whispered. "I guess we've waited long enough."

He eased himself out of the alley and led me in a long circle around the shop, stopping again only when we had returned to our original spot by the alley.

"Well, what do you think, kid?"

"Don't know. What were we looking for?"

"Tell me again about how you planned to be a thief," Aahz sighed. "Look, kid. We're looking over a target. Right?"

"Right," I replied, glad to be able to agree with something.

"Okay, how many ways in and out of that shop did you see?"

"Just one. The one across the street there."

"Right. Now how do you figure we're going to get into the shop?"

"I don't know," I said honestly.

"C'mon, kid. If there's only one way in...."

"You mean we're just going to walk in the front door?"

"Why not? We can see from here the door's open."

"Well...if you say so, Aahz. I just thought it would be harder than that."

"Whoa! Nobody said it was going to be easy. Just because the door's open doesn't mean the door's open."

"I didn't quite get that, Aahz."

"Think, kid. We're after a Deveel, right? He's got access to all kinds of magic and gimmicks. Now what say you close your eyes and take another look at that door."

I did as I was told. Immediately the image of a glowing cage sprang into my mind, a cage that completely enclosed the shop.

"He's got some kind of ward up, Aahz," I informed my partner.

It occurred to me that a few short weeks ago I would have held such a structure in awe. Now, I accepted it as relatively normal, just another obstacle to be overcome.

"Describe it to me," Aahz hissed.

"Well...it's bright...whitish purple...there's a series of bars and crossbars forming squares about a handspan across...."

"Is it just over the door, or all over the shop?"

"All over the shop. The top's covered, and the bars run right into the ground."

"Hmm, well, we'll just have to go through it. Listen up, kid. Time for a quick lesson."

I opened my eyes and looked at the shop again. The building looked as innocent as it had when we first circled it. It bothered me that I couldn't sense the cage's presence the way I could our own wards.

"What is it, Aahz?" I asked uneasily.

"Hmm? Oh, it's a ward, kind of like the ones we use, but a lot nastier."

"Nastier, how?"

"Well, the kind of ward I taught you to build are an early

warning system and not much else. From the sounds of it, the stuff Frumple is using will do considerably more. Not only will it kill you, it'll knock you into pieces smaller than dust. It's called disintegration."

"And we're going to go through it?" I asked, incredulously.

"*After* you've had a quick lesson. Now, remember your feather drills? How you'd wrap your mind around the feather for control?"

"Yeah," I said, puzzled.

"Well, I want you to do the same thing, but without the feather. Pretend you're holding something that isn't there. Form the energies into a tube."

"Then what?"

"Then you insert the tube into one of the squares in the cage and expand it."

"That's all?"

"That's it. C'mon now. Give it a try."

I closed my eyes and reached out with my mind. Choosing a square in the center of the open doorway, I inserted my mental tube and began to expand it. As it touched the bars forming the square, I experienced a tingle and a physical pressure as if I had encountered a tangible object.

"Easy, kid," Aahz said softly. "We just want to bend the bars a bit, not break them."

I expanded the tube. The bars gave way slowly, until they met with the next set. Then I experienced another tingle and additional pressure.

"Remember, kid. Once we're inside, take your time. Wait for your eyes to adjust to the dark. We don't want to tip Frumple off by stumbling around and knocking things over."

I was having to strain now. The tube had reached another set of bars now, making it a total of twelve bars I was forcing outward.

"Have you got it yet?" Aahz's whisper sounded anxious.

"Just a second...Yes!"

The tube was now big enough for us to crawl through.

"Are you sure?"

"Yes."

"Okay. Lead the way, kid. I'll be right behind you."

Strangely enough, I felt none of my usual doubts as I strode boldly across the street to the shop. Apparently my confidence in my abilities was growing, for I didn't even hesitate as I began to crawl through the tube. The only bad moment I had was when I suddenly realized I was crawling on thin air about a foot off the ground. Apparently I had set the tube a little too high, but no matter. It held! Next time I would know better.

I eased myself out of the end of the tube and stood in the shop's interior. I could hear the soft sounds of Aahz's passage behind me as I waited for my eyes to adjust to the dark.

"Ease away from the door, kid," came Aahz's whispered advice in my ear as he stood behind me. "You're standing in a patch of moonlight. And you can collapse the tube now."

Properly notified, I shifted away from the moonlight. I was pleased to note, however, that releasing the tube did not make a significant difference in my mental energies. I was progressing to where I could do more difficult feats with less energy than when I started. I was actually starting to feel like a magician.

I heard a slight noise behind me and craned my neck to look. Aahz was quietly drawing the curtains over the door.

I smiled grimly to myself. Good! We don't want witnesses.

My eyes were nearly adjusted now. I could make out shapes and shadows in the darkness. There was a dark lump in the corner that breathed heavily. Frumple!

I felt a hand on my shoulder. Aahz pointed out a lamp on a table and held up four fingers.

I nodded and started counting slowly to four. As I reached the final number, I focused a quick flash of energy at the lamp, and its wick burst into flame, lighting the shop's interior.

Aahz was kneeling beside Frumple, knife in hand. Apparently he had succeeded in finding at least some of our weapons in the dark.

Frumple sat up blinking, then froze in place. Aahz had the point of his knife hovering a hairsbreadth from the Deveel's throat.

"Hello, Frumple," he smiled. "Remember us?"

"You!" gasped the Deveel. "You're supposed to be dead!"

"Dead?" Aahz purred. "How could any harm befall us with our old pal Frumple helping us blend with the citizenry?"

"Gentlemen!" our victim squealed. "There seems to have been a mistake!"

"That's right," I commented. "And you made it."

"You don't understand!" Frumple persisted, "I was surprised and horrified when I heard about your deaths."

"Yeah, we weren't too happy about it ourselves."

"Later, kid. Look, Frumple. Right now we have both the ability and the motive to kill you. Right?"

"But I...."

"Right?"

Aahz moved the knife until the point was indenting the skin on Frumple's throat.

"Right!" the Deveel whispered.

"Okay, then." Aahz withdrew the knife and tucked it back in his waistband. "Now let's talk business."

"I...I don't understand," Frumple stammered, rubbing his throat with one hand as if to assure himself that it was still there.

"What it means," Aahz explained, "is that we want your help more than we want revenge. Don't relax too much, though. The choice wasn't that easy."

"I...I see. Well, what can I do for you?"

"C'mon, Frumple. You can honor our original deal. You've got to admit we've laid one heck of a false trail for your two fugitives. Now it's your turn. Just restore my powers and we'll be on our way."

The Deveel blanched, or at least he turned from red to pink.

"I can't do that!" he exclaimed.

"What?"

The knife appeared in Aahz's hand again as if by magik.

"Now look, you double-dealing refugee. Either you restore my powers or...."

"You don't understand," Frumple pleaded. "I don't mean I won't restore your powers. I mean I can't. I don't know what's wrong with you or how to counter it. That's why I set you up with the mob. I was afraid if I told you before, you wouldn't believe me. I've spent too much time establishing myself here to risk being exposed by an unsatisfied customer. I'm sorry, I really am, and I know you'll probably kill me, but I can't help you!"

Chapter Sixteen:

"Just because something doesn't do what you planned it to do doesn't mean it's useless."

T. EDISON

"Hmmm," Aahz said thoughtfully. "So you're powerless to restore my powers?"

"Does that mean we can kill him after all?" I asked eagerly. I had been hopeful of having Aahz's powers restored, but in lieu of that, I was still a bit upset over having been hung.

"You're a rather vicious child," Frumple looked at me speculatively. "What's a Pervect doing traveling with a Klahd, anyway?"

"Who's a clod?" I bristled.

"Easy, kid," Aahz said soothingly. "Nothing personal. Everyone who's native to this dimension is a Klahd. Klah...Klahds...get it?"

"Well, I don't like the sound of it," I grumbled.

"Relax, kid. What's in a name, anyway?"

"Then it doesn't really matter to you if people call you a Pervect or a Pervert?"

"Watch your mouth, kid. Things are going bad enough without you getting cheeky."

"Gentlemen, gentlemen," Frumple interrupted. "If you're going to fight would you mind going outside? I mean, this *is* my shop."

"Can we kill him now, Aahz?"

"Ease up, kid. Just because he can't restore my powers doesn't mean he's totally useless. I'm sure that he'll be more than happy to help us, particularly after he failed to pay up on our last deal. Right, Frumple?"

97

"Oh, definitely. Anything I can do to make up for the inconvenience I've caused you."

"Inconvenience?" I asked incredulously.

"Steady, kid. Well, Frumple, you could start by returning the stuff we left here when we went off on your little mission."

"Of course. I'll get it for you."

The Deveel started to rise, only to find Aahz's knife threatening him again.

"Don't trouble yourself, Frumple, old boy," Aahz smiled. "Just point out where they are and we'll fetch them ourselves...and keep you hands where I can see them."

"The...your things are over there...in the big chest against the wall," Frumple's eyes never left the knife as he spoke.

"Check it out, kid."

I did and, surprisingly, the items were exactly where the Deveel said they would be. There was, however, an intriguing collection of other strange items in the chest also.

"Hey, Aahz!" I called. "Take a look at this!"

"Sure, kid."

He backed across the shop to join me. As he did, he flipped the knife into what I now recognized as a throwing grip. Apparently Frumple recognized it too, because he stayed frozen in position.

"Well, what have we here?" Aahz chortled.

"Gentlemen," the Deveel called plaintively. "I could probably help you better if I knew what you needed."

"True enough," Aahz responded, reclaiming his weapons. "Frumple, it occurs to me we haven't been completely open with you. That will have to be corrected if we're going to be allies."

"Wait a minute, Aahz," I interrupted. "What makes you think we can trust him after he's tried so hard to get us killed?"

"Simple, kid. He tried to get us killed to protect himself, right?"

"Well...."

"So once we explain it's in his own self-interest to help us, he should be completely trustworthy."

"Really?" I sneered.

"Well, as trustworthy as any Deveel can be," Aahz admitted.

"I resent the implications of that, Pervert!" Frumple exclaimed. "If you want any help, you'd better...." Aahz's knife flashed through the air and thunked into the wall scant inches from the Deveel's head.

"Shut up and listen, Frumple!" he snarled. "And that's Pervect!"

"What's in a name, Aahz?" I asked innocently.

"Shut up, kid. Okay, Frumple, does the name Isstvan mean anything to you?"

98

"No. Should it?"

"It should if you want to stay alive. He's a madman magician who's trying to take over the dimensions, starting with this one."

"Why should that concern me?" Frumple frowned. "We Deveels trade with anyone who can pay the price. We don't concern ourselves with analyzing politics or mental stability. If we only dealt with sane beings, it would cut our business by a third... maybe more."

"Well, you'd better concern yourself this time. Maybe you didn't hear me. Isstvan is starting with this dimension. He's out to get a monopoly on Klah's energies to use on other dimensions. To do that, he's out to kill anyone else in this dimension who knows how to tap those energies. He's not big on sharing."

"Hmmm. Interesting theory, but where's the proof—I mean, who's he supposed to have killed?"

"Garkin, for one," I said, dryly.

"That's right," Aahz snarled. "You're so eager to know why the two of us are traveling together. Well, Skeeve here was Garkin's apprentice until Isstvan sent his assassins to wipe out the competition."

"Assassins?"

"That's right. You saw two of them, those Imps you teleported about a week back." Aahz flourished the assassin's cloak we had acquired.

"Where did you think we got this? In a rummage sale?"

"Hmmm," Frumple commented thoughtfully.

"And he's arming them with tech weapons. Take a look at this crossbow quarrel."

Aahz lobbed one of the missiles to the Deveel who caught it deftly and examined it closely.

"Hmmm. I didn't notice that before. It's a good camouflage job, but totally unethical."

"Now do you see why enlisting your aid takes priority over the pleasure of slitting your lying throat?"

"I see what you mean," Frumple replied without rancor. "It's most convincing. But what can I do?"

"You tell us. You Deveels are supposed to have wonders for every occasion. What have you got that would give us an edge over a madman who knows his magik?"

Frumple thought for several minutes. Then shrugged. "I can't think of a thing just offhand. I haven't been stocking weapons lately. Not much call for them in this dimension."

"Terrific," I said. "Can we kill him now, Aahz?"

"Say, could you put a muzzle on him?" Frumple said. "What's

your gripe anyway, Skeeve?"

"I don't take well to being hung," I snarled.

"Really? Well, you'll get used to it if you keep practicing magik. It's being burned that's really a pain."

"Wait a minute, Frumple," Aahz interrupted. "You're acting awfully casual about hanging for someone who was so surprised to see us alive."

"I was. I underestimated your apprentice's mastery of the energies. If I had thought you could escape, I would have thought of something else. I *was* trying to get you killed, after all."

"He doesn't sound particularly trustworthy," I observed.

"You will notice, my young friend, that I stated my intentions in the past tense. Now that we share a common goal, you'll find me much easier to deal with."

"Which brings us back to our original question," Aahz asserted. "What can you do for us, Frumple?"

"I really don't know," the Deveel admitted. "Unless...I know! I can send you to the Bazaar!"

"The Bazaar?" I asked.

"The Bazaar on Deva! If you can't find what you need there, it doesn't exist. Why didn't I think of that before? That's the answer!"

He was on his feet now, moving toward us.

"I know you're in a hurry, so I'll get you started...."

"Not so fast, Frumple."

Aahz had his sword out menacing the Deveel.

"We want a guarantee this is a round trip you're sending us on."

"I...I don't understand."

"Simple. You tried to get rid of us once. It occurs to me you might be tempted to send us off to some backwater dimension with no way to get back."

"But I give you my word that...."

"We don't want your word," Aahz grinned. "We want your presence."

"What?"

"Where we go, you go. You're coming with us, just to be extra sure we get back."

"I can't do that!" Frumple seemed honestly terrified. "I've been banned from Deva! You don't know what they'd do to me if I went back."

"That's too bad. We want a guaranteed return before we budge, and that's you!"

"Wait a minute! I think I've got the answer!"

The Deveel began frantically rummaging through chests. I watched, fascinated, as an astounding array of strange objects emerged as he searched.

"Here it is!" he cried at last, holding his prize aloft.

It appeared to be a metal rod, about eight inches long and two inches in diameter. It had strange markings on its sides, and a button on the end.

"A D-Hopper!" Aahz exclaimed. "I haven't seen one of those in years."

Frumple tossed it to him.

"There you go. Is that guarantee enough?"

"What is it, Aahz?" I asked, craning my neck to see.

He seized the ends of the rod and twisted in opposite directions. Apparently it was constructed of at least two parts, because the symbols began to slide around the rod in opposite directions.

"Depending on where you want to go, you align different symbols. Then you just push the button and...."

"Wait a minute!" Frumple cried. "We haven't settled on a price for that yet!"

"Price?" I asked.

"Yeah, price! Those things don't grow on trees, you know."

"If you will recall," Aahz murmured, "you still owe us from our last deal."

"True enough," Frumple agreed. "But as you yourself pointed out, those D-Hoppers are rare. A real collector's item. It's only fair that our contract be renegotiated at a slightly higher fee."

"Frumple, we're in too much of a hurry to argue," Aahz announced. "I'll say once what we're willing to relinquish over and above our original deal and you can take it or leave it. Fair enough?"

"What did you have in mind?" Frumple asked, rubbing his hands together eagerly.

"Your life."

"My...Oh! I see. Yes, that...um...should be an acceptable price."

"I'm surprised at you, Frumple," I chimed in. "Letting a collector's item go that cheap."

"C'mon, kid." Aahz was adjusting the settings on the D-Hopper. "Let's get moving."

"Just a second, Aahz. I want to get my sword."

"Leave it. We can pick it up on the way back."

"Say, Aahz, how long does it take to travel between dimensions any...."

The walls of Frumple's hut suddenly dissolved in a kaleidoscope of color.

"Not long, kid. In fact, we're there."

And we were.

Chapter Seventeen:

"The wonders of the ages assembled for your edification, education, and enjoyment—for a price."

P. T. BARNUM

While I knew my home dimension wasn't particularly colorful, I never really considered it drab...until I first set eyes on the Bazaar at Deva.

Even though both Aahz and Frumple, and even the Imps, had referred to this phenomenon, I had never actually sat back and tried to envision it. It was just as well. Anything I could have fantasized would have been dwarfed by the real thing.

The Bazaar seemed to stretch endlessly in all directions as far as the eye could see. Tents and lean-tos of all designs and colors were gathered in irregular clumps that shoved against each other for more room.

There were thousands of Deveels everywhere of every age and description. Tall Deveels, fat Deveels, lame Deveels, bald Deveels, all moved about until the populace gave the appearance of being one seething mass with multiple heads and tails. There were other beings scattered through the crowd. Some of them looked like nightmares come to life; others I didn't recognize as being alive until they moved, but they all made noise.

The noise! Twixt had seemed noisy to me after my secluded life with Garkin, but the clamor that assailed my ears now defied all description. There were shrieks and dull explosions and strange burbling noises emanating from the depths of the booths around us, competing with the constant din of barter. It seemed no one spoke below a shout. Whether weeping piteously, barking in anger, or displaying bored indifference, all bartering was to be done at the top of your lungs.

"Welcome to Deva, kid," Aahz gestured expansively. "What do you think?"

"It's loud," I observed.

"What?"

"I said, 'it's loud!' " I shouted.

"Oh, well. It's a bit livelier than your average Farmer's Market or Fisherman's Wharf, but there are noisier places to be."

I was about to respond when a passerby careened into me. He, or she, had eyes spaced all around his head and fur-covered tentacles instead of arms.

"Wzklp!" it said, waving a tentacle as it continued on its way.

"Aahz!"

"Yeah, kid?"

"It just occurred to me. What language do they speak on Deva?"

"Hmm? Oh! Don't worry about it, kid. They speak all languages here. No Deveel that's been hatched would let a sale get away just because they couldn't speak the right tongue. Just drop a few sentences on 'em in Klahdish and they'll adapt fast enough."

"Okay, Aahz. Now that we're here, where do we go first?"

There was no answer. I tore my eyes away from the Bazaar and glanced at my partner. He was standing motionless, sniffing the air.

"Aahz?"

"Hey kid, do you smell that?" he asked eagerly.

I sniffed the air.

"Yeah!" I gagged. "What died?"

"C'mon, kid. Follow me."

He plunged off into the crowd, leaving me little choice but to trail after him. Hands plucked at our sleeves as we passed, and various Deveels leaned out of their stalls and tents to call to us as we passed, but Aahz didn't slacken his pace. I couldn't get a clear look at any of the displays as we passed. Keeping up with Aahz demanded most of my concentration. One tent, however, did catch my eye.

"Look, Aazh!" I cried.

"What?"

"It's raining in that tent!"

As if in answer to my words, a boom of thunder and a crackle of lightning erupted from the display.

"Yeah. So?" Aahz dismissed it with a glance.

"What are they selling, rain?"

"Naw. Weather control devices. They're scattered through the whole Bazaar instead of hanging together in one section. Something about the devices interfering with each other."

"Are all the displays that spectacular?"

"That isn't spectacular, kid. They used to do tornados until the other booths complained and they had to limit their demonstrations to the tame stuff. Now hurry up!"

"Where are we going anyway, Aahz? And what is that smell?" The repulsive aroma was growing noticeably stronger.

"That," proclaimed Aahz, coming to a halt in front of a dome-shaped tent, "is the smell of Pervish cooking!"

"Food? We came all this way so you could have a meal?"

"First things first, kid. I haven't had a decent meal since Garkin called me out of the middle of a party and stranded me in your idiot dimension."

"But we're supposed to be looking for something to use against Isstvan."

"Relax, kid. I haggle better on a full stomach. Just wait here. I won't be long."

"Wait here? Can't I go in with you?"

"I don't think you'd like it, kid. To anyone who wasn't born on Perv, the food looks even worse than it smells."

I found that hard to believe, but pursued the argument gamely.

"I'm not all that weak-stomached, you know. When I was living in the woods, I ate some pretty weird things myself."

"I'll tell ya, kid, the main problem with Pervish food is keeping the goo from crawling out of the bowl while you're eating it."

"I'll wait here," I decided.

"Good. Like I say, I won't be long. You can watch the dragons until I get back."

"Dragons?" I said, but he had already disappeared through the tent flap.

I turned slowly and looked at the display behind me.

Dragons!

There was an enormous stall stocked with dragons not fifteen feet from where I was standing. Most of the beasts were tethered at the back wall which kept me from seeing them as we approached, but upon direct viewing there was no doubt they were dragons.

Curiosity made me drift over to join the small crowd in front of the stall. The stench was overwhelming, but after a whiff of Pervish cooking, it seemed almost pleasant.

I had never seen a dragon before, but the specimens in the stall lived up to the expectations of my daydreams. They were huge, easily ten or fifteen feet high at the shoulder and a full thirty feet long. Their necks were long and serpentine, and their clawed feet dug great gouges in the ground as they shifted their weight nervously.

I was surprised to see how many varieties there were. It had never occurred to me that there might be more than one type of dragon, but here was living proof to the contrary. Besides the green dragons I had always envisioned, there were red, black, gold and blue dragons. There was even one that was mauve. Some were winged and some weren't. Some had wide, massive jaws and others had narrow snouts. Some had eyes that were squinting and slanted, while others had huge moonlike eyes that never seemed to blink. They had two things in common, however, they were all big and they all looked thoroughly nasty.

My attention was drawn to the Deveel running the operation. He was the biggest Deveel I had ever seen, fully eight feet tall with arms like trees. It was difficult to say which was more fearsome in appearance, the dragons or their keeper.

He brought one of the red dragons to the center of the stall and released it with a flourish. The beast raised its head and surveyed the crowd with seething yellow eyes. The crowd fell back a few steps before that gaze. I seriously considered leaving.

The Deveel shouted a few words at the crowd in gibberish I couldn't understand, then picked up a sword from the rack by the wall.

Fast as a cat, the dragon arched his neck and spat a stream of fire at its keeper. By some miracle, the flame parted as it hit the Deveel and passed harmlessly on either side of him.

The keeper smiled and turned to shout a few more words at his audience. As he did, the dragon lept at him with murderous intent. The Deveel dove to the ground and rolled out from under the attack as the beast landed with an impact that shook the tent. The dragon whirled, but the keeper was on his feet again, holding aloft a pendant before the beast's eyes.

I didn't understand his move, but apparently the dragon did, for it cowered back on its haunches. The Deveel pointed forcefully and it slunk back to its place at the back of the stall.

A small ripple of applause rippled through the crowd. Apparently they were impressed with the ferocity of the dragon's attack. Me, I was impressed by the pendant.

The keeper acknowledged the applause and launched into another spiel of gibberish, this time punctuated by gestures and exclamations.

I decided it was about time for me to go.

"Gleep!"

There was a tug at my sleeve.

I looked around. There, behind me, was a small dragon! Well, he was about four feet high and ten feet long, but after looking at the other dragons, he seemed small. He was green with big blue eyes and what appeared to be a drooping white mustache.

For a split second I was panicky, but that rapidly gave way to curiosity. He didn't look dangerous. He seemed quite content just standing there chewing on....

My sleeve! The beast was eating a piece of my sleeve! I looked down and confirmed that part of my shirt was indeed missing.

"Gleep," said the dragon again, stretching his neck out for another mouthful.

"Go away!" I said, and cuffed him before I realized what I was doing.

"Gleep?" it said, puzzled.

I started to edge away. I was unsure of what to do if he cut loose with a blast of fire and therefore eager to avoid it.

"Gleep," it said, shuffling after me.

"Gazabkp!" roared a voice behind me.

I spun and found myself looking at a hairy stomach. I followed it up, way up, and saw the dragon keeper's face looming over me.

"I'm sorry," I apologized readily. "I don't speak your language."

"Oh. A Klahd!" The Deveel boomed. "Well, the statement still stands. Pay up!"

"Pay up for what?"

"For the dragon! What do you think, we're giving away samples?"

"Gleep!" said the dragon, pressing his head against my leg.

"There seems to be some mistake," I said hastily.

"I'll say there is," the Deveel scowled. "And you're making it. We don't take kindly to shoplifters on Deva!"

"Gleep!" said the dragon.

Things were rapidly getting out of hand. If I ever needed Aahz's help or advice, it was now. I shot a desperate glance toward the tent he was in, hoping beyond hope to see him emerge.

He wasn't there. In fact, the tent wasn't there! It was gone, vanished into thin air, and so had Aahz!

Chapter Eighteen:

*"No matter what the product or service might be,
you can find it somewhere else cheaper!"*

E. SCROOGE

"Where did that tent go?" I demanded desperately.

"What tent?" The keeper blinked, looming behind me.

"That tent," I exclaimed, pointing at the now vacant space.

The Deveel frowned, craning his neck, which at his height, gave him considerable visibility.

"There isn't any tent there," he announced with finality.

"I know! That's the point!"

"Hey! Quit trying to change the subject!" The keeper growled, poking me in the chest with an unbelievably large finger. "Are you going to pay for the dragon or not?"

I looked around for support, but no one was watching. Apparently disputes such as this were common on Deva.

"I told you there's been a mistake! I don't want your dragon."

"Gleep!" said the dragon, cocking his head at me.

"Don't give me that!" the keeper boomed. "If you didn't want him, why did you feed him?"

"I didn't feed him! He ate a piece of my sleeve!"

"Gleep!" said the dragon, making another unsuccessful pass at my shirt.

"So you admit he got food from you?"

"Well...in a manner of speaking...Yeah! So what?" I was getting tired of being shouted at.

"So pay up! He's no good to me anymore."

I surveyed the dragon. He didn't seem to be any the worse for having eaten the shirt.

"What's wrong with him? He looks all right to me."

"Gleep!" said the dragon, and sidled up to me again.

"Oh! He's fine," the keeper sneered. "Except now he's attached. An attached dragon isn't any good except to the person or thing he's attached to."

"Well, who's he attached to?"

"Don't get smart with me! He's attached to you! Has been ever since you fed him."

"Well, feed him again and unattach him! I have pressing matters elsewhere."

"Just like that, huh?" the Deveel said skeptically, towering to new heights. "You know very well it doesn't work that way. Once a dragon's attached, it's attached forever. That's why they're so valuable."

"Forever?" I asked.

"Well...until one of you dies. But any fool knows not to feed a dragon unless they want it attached to them. The idiot beasts are too impressionable, especially the young ones like this."

I looked at the dragon again. He was very young. His wings were just beginning to bud, which I took as a sign of immaturity, and his fangs were needle-sharp instead of worn to rounded points like his brethren in the stall. Still, there was strength in the muscles rippling beneath those scales...Yes, I decided, I'd back my dragon in a fight against any....

"Gleep!" said the dragon, licking both ends of his mustache simultaneously with his forked tongue.

That brought me to my senses. A dragon? What did I want with a dragon?

"Well," I said haughtily, "I guess I'm not just any fool, then. If I had known the consequences of allowing him to eat my sleeve, I would have..."

"Look, sonny!" The Deveel snarled, poking my chest again. "If you think you're going to...."

Something inside me snapped. I knocked his hand away with a fury that surprised me.

"The name isn't 'Sonny,'" I hissed in a low voice I didn't recognize as my own. "It's Skeeve! Now lower your voice when you're talking to me and keep your dirty finger to yourself!"

I was shaking, though whether from rage or from fear I couldn't tell. I had spent my entire burst of emotion in that outburst, and now found myself wondering if I would survive the aftermath.

Surprisingly, the keeper gave ground a few steps at my tirade, and was now studying me with new puzzlement. I felt a pressure at the back of my legs and risked a glance. The dragon was now crouched behind me, craning his neck to peer around my waist at the keeper.

"I'm sorry." The keeper was suddenly humble and fawning. "I didn't recognize you at first. You said your name was...?"

"Skeeve." I prompted haughtily.

"Skeeve." He frowned thoughtfully. "Strange. I don't remember that name."

I wasn't sure who or what he thought I was, but if I had learned one thing traveling with Aahz, it was to recognize and seize an advantage when I saw one.

"The secrecy surrounding my identity should be a clue in itself, if you know what I mean," I murmured, giving him my best conspiratorial wink.

"Of course," he responded. "I should have realized immediately ...."

"No matter," I yawned. "Now then, about the dragon...."

"Yes. Forgive me for losing my temper, but you can see my predicament."

It seemed strange having someone that immense simpering at me, but I rose to the occasion.

"Well, I'm sure we can work something out," I smiled.

As I spoke, a thought flashed through my head. Aahz had all our money! I didn't have a single item of any value on me except....

I reached into my pocket, forcing myself to make the move casual. It was still there! The charm I had taken from Quigley's statue-body that allowed the wearer to see through spells. I had taken it when Aahz wasn't looking and had kept it hidden in case it might be useful in some crisis. Well, this definitely looked like a crisis!

"Here!" I said, tossing the charm to him. "I believe this should settle our accounts."

He caught it deftly and gave it a fast, squinting appraisal.

"This?" he said. "You want to purchase a hatchling dragon for this?"

I had no idea of the charm's relative worth, but bluffing had gotten me this far.

"I do not haggle," I said coldly. "That is my first and final offer. If it is not satisfactory, then return the charm and see if you can get a better price for an attached dragon."

"You drive a hard bargain, Skeeve." The Deveel was still polite, but his smile looked like it hurt. "Very well, it's a deal. Shake on it."

He extended his hand.

There was a sudden hissing noise and my vision was obscured. The dragon had arched his neck forward over my head and was confronting the Deveel eye-to-eye. His attitude was suddenly a miniature version of the ferocity I had seen displayed earlier by his larger brethren. I realized with a start that he was defending me!

Apparently the keeper realized it too, for he jerked back his hand as if he had just stuck it in an open fire.

"...if you could call off your dragon long enough for us to close the deal?" he suggested with forced politeness.

I wasn't sure just how I was supposed to do this, but I was willing to give it a try.

"He's okay!" I shouted, thumping the dragon on the side of the neck to get his attention.

"Gleep?" said the dragon, turning his head to peer into my face.

I noticed his breath was bad enough to kill an insect in flight.

"It's okay," I repeated, edging out from under his neck.

Since I was already moving, I stepped forward and shook the keeper's hand. He responded absently, never taking his eyes from the dragon.

"Say," I said. "Confidentially, I'm rather new to the dragon game. What does he eat...besides shirts, I mean."

"Oh, a little of this and a little of that. They're omnivorous, so they can eat anything, but they're picky eaters. Just let him alone and he'll choose his own diet...old clothes, selected leaves, house pets."

"Terrific!" I mumbled.

"Well, if you'll excuse me I've got other customers to talk to."

"Just a minute! Don't I get one of those pendants like you used to control the big dragons?"

"Hmm? What for?"

"Well...to control my dragon."

"Those are to control unattached dragons. You don't need one for one that's attached to you and it wouldn't work on a dragon that's attached to someone else."

"Oh," I said, with a wisdom I didn't feel.

"If you want one, though, I have a cousin who has a stall that sells them. It's about three rows up and two rows over. It might be a good investment for you. Could save wear and tear on your dragon if you come up against an unattached dragon. It'd give junior there a better chance of growing up."

"That brings up another question," I said. "How long does it take?"

"Not long. It's just three rows up and...."

"No. I mean how long until my dragon reaches maturity?"

"Oh, not more than four or five centuries."

"Gleep!"

I'm not sure if the dragon said that or I did.

Chapter Nineteen:

"By persevering over all obstacles and distractions, one may unfailingly arrive at his chosen goal or destination."

C. COLUMBUS

"C'mon, Gleep," I said.

"Gleep," my dragon responded, falling in behind me.

Now that I was the not-so-proud owner of a permanently immature dragon, I was more eager than ever to find Aahz. At the moment, I was alone in a strange dimension, penniless, and now I had a dragon tagging after me. The only way things could be worse would be if the situation became permanent, which could happen if Aahz decided to return to Klah without me.

The place previously occupied by the Pervish restaurant tent was definitely empty, even at close examination, so I decided to ask the Deveel running the neighboring booth.

"Um...excuse me, sir."

I decided I was going to be polite as possible for the duration of my stay on Deva. The last thing I needed was another dispute with a Deveel. It seemed, however, in this situation I needn't have worried.

"No excuses are necessary, young sahr." The proprietor smiled eagerly, displaying an impressive number of teeth.

"You are interested in purchasing a stick?"

"A stick?"

"Of course!" the Deveel gestured grandly around his stall. "The finest sticks in all the dimensions."

"Aah...thanks, but we have plenty of sticks in my home dimension."

"Not like these sticks, young sahr. You are from Klah, are you not?"

"Yes, why?"

"I can guarantee you, there are no such sticks as these in all of Klah. They come from a dimension only I have access to and I have not sold them in Klah or to anyone who was going there."

Despite myself, my curiosity was piqued. I looked again at the sticks lining the walls of the stall. They looked like ordinary sticks such as could be found anywhere.

"What do they do?" I asked cautiously.

"Aah! Different ones do different things. Some control animals, others control plants. A few very rare ones allow you to summon an army of warriors from the stones themselves. Some of the most powerful magicians of any dimension wield staffs of the same wood as these sticks, but for most people's purposes the smaller model will suffice."

"Gleep!" said the dragon, sniffing at one of the sticks.

"Leave it alone!" I barked, shoving his head away from the display.

All I needed was to have my dragon eat up the entire stock of one of these super-merchants.

"May I inquire, is that your dragon, young sahr?"

"Well...sort of."

"In that case, you might find a particular use for a stick most magicians wouldn't."

"What's that?"

"You could use it to beat your dragon."

"Gleep!" said the dragon, looking at me with his big blue eyes.

"Actually, I'm not really interested in a stick."

I thought I'd better get to my original purpose before this conversation got out of hand.

"Ridiculous, young sahr. Everybody should have a stick."

"The reason I stopped here in the first place is I wondered if you knew what happened to that tent."

"What tent, young sahr?"

I had a vague feeling of having had this conversation before.

"The tent that was right there next to your stall."

"The Pervish restaurant!?" The Deveel's voice was tinged with horror.

"Gleep," said the dragon.

"Why would you seek such place, young sahr? You seem well-bred and educated."

"I had a friend who was inside the tent when it vanished."

"You have a Pervert for a friend?" His voice had lost it's friendly tone.

114

"Well actually...um...it's a long story."

"I can tell you this much, punk. It didn't disappear, it moved on," the Deveel snarled, without the accent or politeness he had displayed earlier.

"Moved on?"

"Yeah. It's a new ordinance we passed. All places serving Pervish food have to migrate. They cannot be established permanently, or even temporarily at any point in the Bazaar."

"Why?" I asked.

"Have you ever smelled Pervish food? It's enough to make a scavenger nauseous. Would you want to man a stall down wind of that for a whole day? In this heat?"

"I see what you mean," I admitted.

"Either they moved or the Bazaar did, and we have them outnumbered."

"But what exactly do you mean, move?"

"The tents! All that's involved is a simple spell or two. Either they constantly move at a slow pace, or they stay in one place for a short period and then scuttle off to a new location, but they all move."

"How does anyone find one, then, if they keep moving around?"

"That's easy, just follow your nose."

I sniffed the air experimentally. Sure enough, the unmistakable odor was still lingering in the air.

"Gleep!" the dragon had imitated my action and was now rubbing his nose with one paw.

"Well, thank you...for...your...."

I was talking to thin air. The Deveel was at the other end of the stall, baring his teeth at another customer. It occurred to me that the citizens of Deva were not particularly concerned with social pleasantries beyond those necessary to transact a sale.

I set out to follow the smell of the Pervish restaurant with the dragon faithfully trailing along behind. Despite my growing desire to reunite with Aahz, my pace was considerably slower than that Aahz had set when we first arrived. I was completely mezmerized by this strange Bazaar and wanted to see as much of it as I could.

Upon more leisurely examination, there did seem to be a vague order to the Bazaar. The various stalls and booths were generally grouped by type of merchandise. This appeared to be more from circumstance than by plan. Apparently, if one Deveel set up a display, say, of invisible cloaks, in no time at all he had a pack of competitors in residence around him, each vying to top the other for quality of goods or prices. Most of the confused babble of voices were disputes between the merchants over the location of their respective stalls or the space occupied by the same.

The smell grew stronger as I wandered through an area specializing in exotic and magical jewelry, which I resisted the temptation to examine more closely. The temptation was even stronger as I traversed an area which featured weaponry. It occurred to me that I might find a weapon here we could use against Isstvan, but the smell of the Pervish food was even stronger now, and I steeled myself to finish my search. We could look for a weapon after I found Aahz. From the intensity of the stench, I was sure we would find our objective soon.

"C'mon, Gleep," I encouraged.

The dragon was hanging back now and didn't respond except to speed his pace a bit.

I expectantly rounded one last corner and came to an abrupt halt. I had found the source of the odor.

I was looking at the back of a large display of some alien livestock. There was a large pile of some moist green and yellow substance in front of me. As I watched, a young Deveel emerged from the display holding a shovel filled with the same substance. He glanced at me quizzically as he heaved the load onto the pile and returned to the display.

A dung heap! I had been following the smell of a dung heap!

"Gleep!" said the dragon, looking at me quizzically.

He seemed to be asking me what we were going to do next. That was a good question.

I stood contemplating my next move. Probably the best chance would be to retrace our step back to the stick seller and try again.

"Spare a girl a little time, handsome?"

I whirled around. A girl was standing there, a girl unlike any I had ever seen before. She was Klahdish in appearance and could have passed for another of my dimension except for her complexion and hair. Her skin was a marvelous golden-olive hue, and her head was crowned with a mane of light green hair that shimmered in the sun. She was a little taller than me and incredibly curvaceous, her generous figure straining against the confines of her clothes.

"...or have you really got a thing about dung heaps?" she concluded.

She had almond cat-eyes that danced with mischief as she talked.

"Um...are you talking to me?" I stammered.

"Of course I'm talking to you," she purred, coming close to me and twining her arms around my neck. "I'm certainly not talking to your dragon. I mean, he's cute and all, but my tastes don't run in those directions."

"Gleep!" said the dragon.

I felt my body temperature soar. The touch of her arms caused a tingling sensation which seemed to wreak havoc on my metabolism.

"Um...actually I'm looking for a friend," I blurted.

"Well, you've found one," she murmured, moving her body against me.

"Aah...I...um." Suddenly I was having trouble concentrating. "What is it you want?"

"Hmm," she said thoughtfully, "Even though it's not my normal time, I think I'd like to tell your fortune...free."

"Oh?" I said, surprised.

This was the first time since I reached the Bazaar that anyone had offered me anything for free. I didn't know if I should be happy or suspicious.

"You're going to have a fight," she whispered in my ear. "A big one."

"What?" I exclaimed. "When? With who?"

"Easy, handsome," she warned, tightening her grip around my neck. "When is in a very few minutes. With who is the rat pack over my shoulder... don't look right at them!"

Her final sharp warning checked my reflexive glance. Moving more cautiously, I snuck a peek out of the corner of my eye.

Lounging against a shop wall, watching us closely, were a dozen or so of the ugliest, nastiest looking characters I have ever seen.

"Them? I mean, all of them?" I asked.

"Uh-huh!" she confirmed, snuggling into my chest.

"Why?" I demanded.

"I probably shouldn't tell you this," she smiled, "but because of me."

Only her firm grip on me kept me from dislodging her with a shove.

"You? What about you?"

"Well, they're an awfully greedy bunch. One way or another, they're going to make some money from this encounter. Normally, you'd give the money to me and I'd cut them in for a share. In the unlikely event that doesn't work, they'll pretend to be defending my honor and beat it out of you."

"But you don't understand! I don't have any money."

"I know that. That's why you're going to get into a fight, see?"

"If you knew I didn't have any money, why did you...."

"Oh, I didn't know when I first stopped you. I found out just now when I searched you."

"Searched me?"

"Oh, come on, handsome. There's more ways to search a person than with your hands," she winked knowingly at me.

"Well, can't you tell them I don't have any money?"

"They wouldn't believe me. The only way they'd be convinced is searching you themselves."

"I'd be willing to let them if that's what it takes to convince them."

"I don't think you would," she smiled, stroking my face with her hand. "One of the things they'll look for is if you swallowed your money."

"Oh!" I said, "I see what you mean. But I can't fight them. I don't have any weapons."

"You have that little knife under your shirt at the small of your back," she pointed out.

I had forgotten about my skinning knife. I started to believe in her no-hands frisking technique.

"But I've never been in a fight before."

"Well, I think you're about to learn."

"Say, why are you telling me all this, anyway?" I asked.

"I don't know," she shrugged. "I like your act. That's why I singled you out in the first place. Then again, I feel a little guilty about having gotten you into this."

"Will you help me?"

"I don't feel *that* guilty, handsome," she smiled. "But there is one more thing I can do for you."

She started to pull me toward her.

"Wait a minute," I protested. "Won't that...."

"Relax, handsome," she purred. "You're about to get pounded for offending my honor. You might as well get a little of the sweet along with the bitter."

Before I could protest further, she kissed me. Long and warm and sweet, she kissed me.

I had never been kissed by anyone except my mother. This was different! The fight, the dragon, Aahz, everything faded from my mind. I was lost in the wonder of that moment.

"Hey!"

A rough hand fell on my shoulder and pulled us apart.

"Is this shrimp bothering you, lady?"

The person on the other end of that hand was no taller than I was, but he was twice as broad and had short, twisted tusks protruding from his mouth. His cronies had fanned out behind him, effectively boxing me in against the dung-heap.

I looked at the girl. She shrugged and backed away.

It looked like I was going to have to fight all of them. Me and the dragon. Terrific.

I remembered my skinning knife. It wasn't much, but it was all I had. As casually as I could, I reached behind me and tugged at my shirt, trying to pull it up so I could get at the knife. The knife promptly fell down inside my pants.

The wrecking crew started forward.

Chapter Twenty:

"With the proper consideration in choice of allies,
victory may be guaranteed in any conflict."

B. ARNOLD

"Get 'em, Gleep!" I barked.

The dragon bounded into action, a move which I think surprised me more than it did my assailants.

It leaped between me and the advancing rat-pack and crouched there, hissing menacingly. His tail gave a mighty lash which neatly swept the legs out from under two of the flanking members of the party. Somehow, he seemed much bigger when he was mad.

"Watch out! He's got a dragon!" the leader called.

"Thanks for the warning!" one of the fallen men growled, struggling to regain his feet.

"I've got him!" came a voice from my left.

I turned just in time to see a foot-long dagger flashing through the air at the dragon's neck. My dragon!

Suddenly I was back at the practice sessions. My mind darted out and grabbed at the knife. It jerked to a halt in mid-air and hovered there.

"Nice move, handsome!" the girl called.

"Hey! The shrimp's a magician!"

The pack fell back a few steps.

"That's right!" I barked. "Skeeve's the name, magik's the game. What kind of clod did you think you were dealing with?"

With that, I brought the dagger down, swooping it back and forth through their formation. I was mad now. One of these louts had tried to kill my dragon!

"A dozen of you isn't enough!" I shouted. "Go back and get some friends...if you have any!"

I cast about desperately for something else to throw. My eyes fell on the dung-heap. I smiled to myself despite my anger. Why not?

In a moment I had great gobs of dung hurtling through the air at my assailants. My accuracy wasn't the best, but it was good enough as the outraged howls testified.

"Levitation!" the leader bawled. "Quanto! Stop him!"

"Right, boss!"

One of the plug-uglies waved in affirmation and started rummaging through his belt pouch.

He had made a mistake identifying himself. I didn't know what he was about to come up with, but I was sure I didn't want to wait and find out.

"Stop him, Gleep!" I ordered, pointing to the victim.

The dragon raised his head and fixed his gaze on the fumbling brigand. With a sound that might have been a roar if he were older, he shot a stream of flame and charged.

It wasn't much of a stream of flame, and it missed to boot, but it was enough to get the brigand's attention. He looked up to see a mountain of dragon flesh bearing down on him and panicked. Without pausing to call to his comrades, he spun and ran off screaming with the dragon in hot pursuit.

"Okay, shrimp! Let's see you stop this!"

I jerked my attention back to the leader. He was standing now, confidently holding aloft a stick. Yesterday it wouldn't have fazed me, but knowing what I did now, I froze. I didn't know what model it was, but apparently the leader was confident its powers would surpass my own.

He grinned evilly and slowly began to level the stick at me.

I tried desperately to think of a defense, but couldn't. I didn't even know what I was supposed to be defending against!

Suddenly, something flashed across my line of vision and the stick was gone.

I blinked and looked again. The stick was lying on the ground, split by a throwing knife, a black-handled throwing knife.

"Any trouble here, Master Skeeve?" a voice boomed.

I spun toward the source of the voice. Aahz was standing there, cocked crossbow leveled at the pack. He was grinning broadly, which I have mentioned before is not that comforting to anyone who doesn't know him.

"A Pervert!" the leader gasped.

"What?" Aahz swung the crossbow toward him.

"I mean a Pervect!" the leader amended hastily.

"That's better. How about it, Skeeve? You want 'em dead or running?"

I looked at the rat pack. Without breaking their frozen tableau, they pleaded with me with their eyes.

"Um...running, I think," I said thoughtfully. "They smell bad enough alive. Dead they might give the Bazaar a bad name."

"You heard him," Aahz growled. "Move!"

They disappeared like they had melted into the ground.

"Aahz!"

The girl came flying forward to throw her arms around him.

"Tanda!" Aahz exclaimed, lowering the crossbow. "Are you mixed up with that pack?"

"Are you kidding? I'm the bait!" she winked bawdily.

"Little low class for you, isn't it?"

"Aah...it's a living."

"Why'd you leave the Assassins?"

"Got tired of paying union dues."

"Um...harrumph...." I interrupted.

"Hmm?" Aahz looked around. "Oh! Sorry, kid. Say, have you two met?"

"Sort of," the girl acknowledged. "We...say, is this the friend you were looking for, handsome?"

"Handsome?" Aahz wrinkled his nose.

"Well, yes," I admitted. "We got separated back by the...."

"Handsome?" Aahz repeated.

"Oh, hush!" the girl commanded, slapping his stomach playfully. "I like him. He's got style."

"Actually, I don't believe we've met formally," I said, giving my most winning smile. "My name is Skeeve."

"Well, la-de-dah!" Aahz grumbled.

"Ignore him. I'm Tananda, but call me Tanda."

"Love to," I leered.

"If you two are quite through...." Aahz interrupted. "I have a couple questions...."

"Gleep!" said the dragon, prancing up to our assemblage.

"What's that?" Aahz demanded.

"It's a dragon," I said helpfully.

Tanda giggled rudely.

"I know that," Aahz barked. "I mean what is he doing here?"

Suddenly I was hesitant to supply the whole story.

"There are lots of dragons at the Bazaar, Aahz," I mumbled, not looking at him. "In fact, there's a stall just down the way that...."

"What is *that* dragon doing *here*?"

"Gleep!" said the dragon, rubbing his head against my chest.

"Um...he's mine," I admitted.

"Yours?" Aahz bellowed. "I told you to look at the dragons, not buy one!"

"But Aahz...."

"What are we going to do with a dragon?"

"I got a good deal on him," I chimed hopefully.

"What did you say, kid?"

"I said I got a good deal...."

"From a Deveel?"

"Oh. I see what you mean."

"C'mon. Let's have it. What were the terms of this fantastic deal?"

"Well...I...that is...."

"Out with it!"

"I traded Quigley's pendant for him."

"Quigley's pendant? The one that sees through spells? You traded a good magical pendant for a half-grown dragon?"

"Oh, give him a break, Aahz," Tanda interrupted. "What do you expect letting him wander off alone that way? You're lucky he didn't get stuck with half the tourist crud on Deva! Where were you all this time, anyway?"

"Well...I was...um...."

"Don't tell me," she said, holding up a hand. "If I know you, you were either chasing a girl or stuffing your face, right?"

"She's got you there, Aahz," I commented.

"Shut up, kid."

"...so don't get down on Skeeve here. Compared to what could have happened to him, he didn't do half bad. How did you find us, anyway?"

"I listened for the sounds of a fight and followed it," Aahz admitted.

"See! You were expecting him to get into trouble. Might I point out he was doing just fine before you barged in. He and his dragon had those thugs treed all by themselves. He's pretty handy with that magik, you know."

"I know," Aahz responded proudly. "I taught him."

"Gee, thanks, Aahz."

"Shut up, kid."

"Gleep," said the dragon, craning his neck around to look at Aahz upside down.

"A dragon, huh?" Aahz said, studying the dragon more thoughtfully.

"He might help us against Isstvan," I suggested hopefully.

"Isstvan?" Tanda asked quizzically.

"Yeah," Aahz replied. "You remember him, don't you? Well, he's up to his old tricks, this time in Klah."

"So that's what's going on, huh? Well, what are we going to do about it?"

"We?" I asked surprised.

"Sure," she smiled. "This racket is a bit low class like Aahz says. I might as well tag along with you two for a while...if you don't mind, that is."

"Terrific!" I said, and meant it for a change.

"Not so fast, Tanda," Aahz cautioned. "There are a few details you haven't been filled in on yet."

"Such as?"

"Such as I've lost my powers."

"No fooling? Gee, that's tough."

"That means we'll be relying on the kid here to give us cover in the magik department."

"All the more reason for me to come along. I've picked up a few tricks myself."

"I know," Aahz leered.

"Not like that," she said, punching him in the side. "I mean magik tricks."

"Even so, it's not going to be easy."

"C'mon, Aahz," Tanda chided. "Are you trying to say it wouldn't be helpful having a trained Assassin on your side?"

"Well...it could give us a bit of an advantage," Aahz admitted.

"Good! Then it's settled. What do we do first?"

"There're some stalls just around the corner that carry weapons," I suggested. "We could...."

"Relax, kid. I've already taken care of that."

"You have?" I asked, surprised.

"Yeah. I found just what we need over in the practical jokes section. I was just looking for you before we headed back."

"Then we're ready to go?" Tanda asked.

"Yep," Aahz nodded, fishing the D-Hopper out of his shirt.

"What about my dragon?"

"What about him?"

"Are we going to take him with us?"

"Of course we're going to take him with us. We don't leave anything of value behind."

"Gleep!" said the dragon.

"...and he must be valuable to someone!" Aahz finished, glaring at the dragon.

He pressed the button on the D-Hopper. The Bazaar wavered and faded...and we were back in Frumple's shop...sort of.

"Interesting place you've got here," Tanda commented dryly. "Did you do the decor?"

All that was left of Frumple's shop was a burnt-out shell.

Chapter Twenty-One:

"One must deal openly and fairly with one's forces if maximum effectiveness is to be achieved."

D. VADER

"What happened?" I demanded of Aahz.

"Hey, kid. I was on Deva, too. Remember?"

"Um...hey, guys. I hate to interrupt," Tanda interrupted, "but shouldn't something be done about disguises?"

She was right. Being on Deva had made me forget the mundane necessities of our existence. I ignored Aahz's sarcastic reply and set to work.

Aahz returned to his now traditional Garkin disguise. Tanda was fine once I changed her complexion and the color of her hair. After a bit of thought, I disguised Gleep as the war unicorn. It was a bit risky, but it would do as long as he kept his mouth shut. Me, I left as myself. I mean, what the heck. Tanda liked my looks the way they were.

Fortunately the sun wasn't up yet, so there weren't any people about to witness the transformation.

"Say, handsome," Tanda commented, observing the results of my work, "you're a pretty handy guy to have around."

"His name's Skeeve," Aahz grumbled.

"Whatever," Tanda murmured. "He's got style."

She snuggled up to me.

"Gleep!" said the dragon, pressing his head against my other side.

I was starting to feel awfully popular.

"If you can spare a few minutes, kid," Aahz commented dryly, "we do have a mission, remember?"

"That's right," I said, forcing my attention away from Tanda's advances. "What do you think happened to Frumple?"

"Either the citizens of Twixt got wise to him, or he's off to tell Isstvan we're coming, would be my two guesses."

"Who's Frumple?" Tanda asked.

"Hmm? Oh, he's the resident Deveel," Aahz said. "He's the one who helped us get to the Bazaar."

"...at sword point," I added sarcastically.

"What's a Deveel doing here?"

"All we know is that rumor has it he was barred from Deva," I told her.

"Hmm...sounds like a bit of a nasty character."

"Well, he won't win any popularity contests."

"It occurs to me," Aahz interrupted, "that if either of my two guesses are correct, we'd best be on our way. Time seems to be running out."

"Right," agreed Tanda. "Which way is Isstvan?"

"First, we've got to pick up Quigley," I inserted.

"Why?" asked Aahz. "Oh, I suppose you're right, kid. We're going to need all the help we can muster."

"Who's Quigley?" Tanda asked.

"Later, Tanda," Aahz insisted. "First help us see if there's anything here worth salvaging."

Unfortunately, there wasn't. In fact, there weren't even the charred remains of anything left for our discovery. Even the garish sword I had left behind seemed to have vanished.

"That settles it," Aahz commented grimly as we completed our search. "He's on his way to Isstvan."

"The natives might have taken the sword after they burned the place," I suggested hopefully.

"No way, kid. Even yokels like these wouldn't bother with a crummy sword like that."

"It was that bad?" Tanda asked.

"It was that bad," Aahz assured her firmly.

"If it was that worthless, why would Frumple take it with him?" I asked.

"For the same reason we've been lugging it around," Aahz said pointedly. "There's always some sucker to unload it on for a profit. Remember Quigley?"

"Who's Quigley?" Tanda insisted.

"Well," sighed Aahz, "at the moment he's a statue, but in duller times he's a demon hunter."

"Swell," she commented sarcastically. "Just what we need."

"Wait until you meet him," Aahz rolled his eyes and sighed. "Oh well, let's go."

Our departure from Twixt was blissfully uneventful. On the road, we rehearsed our story until by the time we finally dug up Quigley and sprinkled him with the restoring powder, we were ready to present a united front.

"Really? Turned to stone, you say?" he said, brushing the dirt from his clothes.

"Yes," Aahz assured him. "They were looting your body when we launched our counterattack. It's lucky for you we decided to come back and fight at your side."

"And they took my magik sword and my amulet?"

I felt a little uneasy on those subjects, but Aahz never batted an eye.

"That's right, the blackguards!" he snarled. "We tried to stop them, but they eluded us."

"Well, at least they didn't get my war unicorn," muttered the demon-hunter.

"Um...." I said, bracing myself for my part in this charade. "We've got some bad news about that, too."

"Bad news?" Quigley frowned, "I don't understand. I can see the beast with my own eyes and he seems fit enough."

"Oh, he's fine physically," Aahz reassured him, "but before they disappeared, the demons put a spell on him."

"A spell?"

"Yes," I said. "Now he...um...well...he thinks he's a dragon."

"A dragon?" Quigley exclaimed.

"Gleep!" said the dragon.

"And that's not all," Aahz continued. "The beast was so wild at first that only through the continued efforts of my squire here were we able to gentle him at all. Frankly, I was for putting the poor animal out of its misery, but he insisted he could tame it and you see before you the results of his patient teachings."

"That's wonderful!" exclaimed Quigley.

"No. That's terrible," corrected Aahz. "You see, in the process, your animal has formed a strong attachment for my squire... stronger, I fear, than his attachment for you."

"Hah! Ridiculous," Quigley proclaimed. "But I do feel I owe you an additional debt of gratitude, lad. If there's ever anything I can..."

He began to advance on me with his hand extended. In a flash, Gleep was between us, head down and hissing.

Quigley froze, his eyes bulging with surprise.

"Stop that!" I ordered, cuffing the dragon.

"Gleep!" said the dragon, slinking back to his place behind me.

"See what I mean?" Aahz said pointedly.

"Hmm...." Quigley mumbled thoughtfully. "That's strange, he never defended me that way."

"I guess we'll just have to buy him from you," I said eagerly.

"Buy him?" Quigley turned his attention to me again.

Aahz tried to catch my eye, shaking his head emphatically, but I ignored him.

"That's right," I continued. "He's no good to you this way, and since we're sort of to blame for what happened to him...."

"Think nothing of it, lad." Quigley drew himself up proudly. "I give him to you as a gift. After all, if it weren't for you he'd be dead anyway, and so would I, for that matter."

"But I...."

"No! I will hear nothing more." The demon hunter held up a restraining hand. "The matter is closed. Treat him well, lad. He's a good animal."

"Terrific," muttered Aahz.

"Gleep," said the dragon.

I felt miserable. It had occurred to me that our plans involved taking shameless advantage of Quigley's gullibility. As he was my only fellow Klahd in this adventure, I had wanted to force Aahz into giving him some money under the guise of buying the "war unicorn." It would have salved my conscience a bit, but Quigley's generosity and sense of fair play had ruined my plan. Now I felt worse than before.

"Actually, Quigley," Aahz smiled, "If there's anyone you should thank, it should be Tananda here. If it were not for her, we would be in dire straits indeed."

"It's about time," mumbled Tanda, obviously unimpressed with Aahz's rhetoric.

"Charmed, milady," Quigley smiled, taking her hand to kiss.

"She's a witch," added Aahz casually.

"A witch?" Quigley dropped her hand as if it had bitten him.

"That's right, sugar," Tanda smiled, batting her eyes at him.

"Perhaps I should explain," Aahz interrupted mercifully. "Tananda here has certain powers she has consented to use in support of our war on demons. You already noticed I have regained my normal appearance?"

Another blatant lie. Aahz was currently disguised as Garkin.

"Yes," the demon hunter admitted hesitantly.

"Tananda's work," Aahz confided. "Just as it was her powers that restored you after you had been turned to stone."

"Hmmm...." Quigley said, looking at Tanda again.

"Really, you must realize, Quigley, that when one fights

demons, sometimes it is helpful to employ a demon's weapons," Aahz admonished gently.

"Tananda here can be a powerful ally...and frankly, I find your attitude toward her deplorable and ungrateful."

"Forgive me, milady," Quigley sighed, stepping up to her again. "I did not mean to offend you. It's just that... well... I've had some bad experiences with those who associate with demons."

"Think nothing of it, sugar," said Tanda the demon, taking his hand, "And call me Tanda."

While they were occupied with each other, I seized the opportunity and snagged Aahz's arm.

"Hm? What is it, kid?"

"Give him back his sword!" I hissed.

"What? No way, kid. By my count he's still got five pieces of gold left. I'll sell it to him."

"But he gave us his unicorn."

"He gave us a dragon... your dragon! I fail to see anything benevolent in that."

"Look, Aahz. Either you give him that sword or you can work you own magik! Get me?"

"Talk about ingratitude! Look kid, if you...."

"Aahz!" Tanda's voice interrupted our dispute. "Come help me convince Quigley to join our mission."

"Would that I could, milady," Quigley sighed, "but I would be of little help. This late misfortune has left me afoot, weaponless, and penniless."

"Actually," Aahz chimed, "you still have five...."

I interrupted him with an elbow in his ribs.

"What was that, Aahz?" Quigley asked.

"Aah...my...um...squire and I were just discussing that and we have reached a decision. So...um...so fine a warrior should not be left so destitute, so...um...we...."

"We've decided to give you back your sword," I announced proudly.

"Really?" Quigley's face lit up.

"I didn't know you had it in you, Aahz," Tanda smiled sweetly.

"I say, this is comradeship indeed." Quigley was obviously beside himself with joy. "How can I ever repay you?"

"By never mentioning this to anyone," Aahz growled.

"How's that again?"

"I said don't mention it," Aahz amended. "It's the least we can do."

"Believe him," I smiled.

"Now I will gladly assist you on your mission," Quigley

answered. "Why, with a weapon and good comrades, what more could a warrior ask for?"

"Money," Aahz said bluntly.

"Oh Aahz." Tanda punched him a little too hard for it to be playful. "You're such a kidder."

"Don't you want to know what the mission is?" I asked Quigley.

"Oh, yes, I suppose you're right, lad. Forgive me. I was carried away by my enthusiasm."

"Tell him, Skeeve," prompted Tanda.

"Actually," I said, with a sudden flash of diplomacy, "Aahz explains it much better than I do."

"It's really quite simple," mumbled Aahz, still sulking a bit. "We're going after Isstvan."

"Isstvan?" Quigley looked puzzled. "The harmless old innkeeper?"

"Harmless? Harmless, did you say?" Aahz took the bait. "Quigley, as one demon-hunter to another, you've got a lot to learn."

"I do all right for myself."

"Sure you do. That's why you got turned to stone, remember?"

"I got turned to stone because I put my faith in a magik-sword that...."

Things were back to normal.

"Gentlemen, gentlemen," I interrupted. "We were talking about the upcoming mission."

"Right, kid. As I was saying, Quigley, that harmless old innkeeper is working so closely with demons I wouldn't be surprised to learn he was one himself."

"Impossible!" scoffed Quigley. "Why, the man sent me out hunting for demons."

"Ahh!" smiled Aahz. "Therein lies the story."

I caught Tanda's eyes and winked. She smiled back at me and nodded. This might take a while, but as of now Quigley was in the bag!

Chapter Twenty-Two:

"This is another fine myth you've gotten me into!"
Lor L. and Har D.

There was something there in the shadows. I could sense its presence more than see it. It was dark and serpentine... and it was watching me.

I was alone. I didn't know where the others had gone, but I knew they were counting on me.

"Who's there?" I called.

The voice that came back to me out of the darkness echoed hollowly.

"I am Isstvan, Skeeve. I've been waiting for you."

"You know who I am?" I asked, surprised.

"I know all about you and your friends. I've known all along what you're trying to do."

I tried to set wards about me, but I couldn't find a force line. I tried to run, but I was rooted to the spot.

"See how my powers dwarf yours? And you expected to challenge me."

I tried to fight back a wave of despair.

"Wait until the others come," I cried defiantly.

"They already have," the voice boomed. "Look!"

Two objects came rolling at me out of the darkness. I saw with horror that they were heads! Tanda's and Quigley's!

I felt ill, but clung to a shred of hope. There was still no sign of Aahz. If he was still at large, we might....

"Don't look to your Pervert for help," the voice answered my

thoughts. "I've dealt with him too."

Aahz appeared, sheathed in fire. He staggered and fell, writhing on the ground as the flames consumed his body.

"Now it's just you and me, Skeeve!" the voice echoed. "You and me."

"I'll go!" I shouted desperately. "You've won. Just let me go." The darkness was moving closer.

"It's too late. I'm coming for you Skeeve... Skeeve...."

"Skeeve!"

Something was shaking my shoulder. I bolted upright, blinking my eyes as the world swam back into focus.

The camp was asleep. Aahz was kneeling beside me, the glow from the campfire's dying embers revealing the concerned expression on his face.

"Wake up, kid! If you keep thrashing around, you'll end up in the fire."

"It's Isstvan!" I explained desperately. "He knows all about us."

"What?"

"I was talking to him. He came into my dream!"

"Hmmm... sounds more like a plain old nightmare," Aahz proclaimed. "I warned you not to let Tanda season the food."

"Are you sure?" I said doubtfully.

"Positive," Aahz insisted. "If Isstvan knew we were coming, he'd hit us with something a lot more powerful than making faces at you in a dream."

I guess that was supposed to reassure me. It didn't. All it did was remind me I was thoroughly outclassed in the upcoming campaign.

"Aahz, can't you tell me anything about Isstvan? What he looks like for instance."

"Not a chance, kid," Aahz grinned at me.

"Why not?"

"Because we won't both see him the same way, or at least we wouldn't describe him the same way. If I describe him to you, one of two things will happen when you first see him. If he looks scarier to you than I've described him, you'll freeze. If he looks more harmless than I've described him, you'll relax. Either way, it'll slow your reactions and give him the first move. There's no point in gaining the element of surprise if we aren't going to use it."

"Well," I persisted. "Couldn't you at least tell me about his powers? What can he do?"

"For one thing, it would take too long. Just assume that if you can imagine it, he can do it."

"What's the other?" I asked.

"The other what?"

"You said 'for one thing.' That implies you have at least one other reason."

"Hmm," Aahz pondered. "Well, I'm not sure you'll understand, but to a certain degree what he can do, I mean the whole list, is irrelevant."

"Why?"

"Because we're taking the initiative. That puts him in a reactive instead of an active role."

"You're right," I said thoughtfully. "I don't understand."

"Look kid, if we just sat here and waited for him, he could take his time and choose exactly what he wanted to do and when he wanted to do it. That's an active role and lets him play with his entire list of powers. Right?"

"I guess so."

"But we aren't doing that. We're carrying the attack to him. That should limit him as to what he can do. There are only a certain number of responses he can successfully use to each of our gambits, and he'll have to use them because he can't afford to ignore the attack. Most of all, we'll rob him of time. Instead of leisurely choosing what he's going to do next, he'll have to choose fast. That mean's he'll go with the option he's surest of, the one he does best."

I considered this for a few moments. It sort of made sense.

"Just one question, Aahz," I asked finally.

"What's that, kid?"

"What if you've guessed wrong?"

"Then we drop back ten and punt," he answered lightly.

"What's a...."

"Then we try something else," he amended hastily.

"Like what?"

"Can't tell yet," Aahz shrugged. "Too many variables. We're going with my best guess right now. Beyond that we'll just have to wait and see."

We sat staring into the dying fire for a few minutes, each lost in our own thoughts.

"Say, Aahz?" I said at last.

"Yea, kid?"

"Do you think we'll reach Isstvan before Frumple does?"

"Relax, kid. Frumple's probably drinking wine and pinching bottoms in some other dimension by now."

"But you said...."

"I've had time to think about it since then. The only reason a Deveel does anything is for a profit or out of fear. As far as his sticking his head into this brawl goes, I figure the fear will outweigh

135

the profit. Trying to sell information to a madman is risky at best. My bet is he's lying low until the dust settles."

I reminded myself again of my faith in Aahz's expertise in such matters. It occurred to me, however, there was an awful lot of guesswork in our planning.

"Um, Aahz? Wouldn't it be a little safer if we had invested in a couple of those jazzy weapons back in Deva?"

"We don't need them," he replied firmly. "Besides, they're susceptible to Gremlins. I'd rather go into a fight with a crude but reliable weapon than pin my hopes on a contraption that's liable to malfunction when you need it most."

"Where are Gremlins from?" I asked.

"What?"

"Gremlins. You said...."

"Oh, that. It's just a figure of speech. There are no such things as Gremlins."

I was only listening with half an ear. I suddenly realized that while I could see Quigley's sleeping form, there was no sign of Tanda or Gleep.

"Where's... um... where's Gleep?" I asked abruptly.

Aahz grinned at me.

"Gleep is standing watch... and just in case you're interested, so's Tanda."

I was vaguely annoyed he had seen through me so easily, but was determined not to show it.

"When is... um... are they coming back?"

"Relax, kid. I told Tanda to leave you alone tonight. You need the sleep for tomorrow."

He jerked his head pointedly toward the assassin's robe I had been using for a pillow. I grudgingly resumed my horizontal position.

"Did I wake you up, Aahz?" I asked apologetically "With the nightmare, I mean."

"Naw. I was still up. Just making a few last minute preparations for tomorrow."

"Oh," I said drowsily.

"Say, uh, kid?"

"Yes, Aahz?"

"We probably won't have much time to talk tomorrow when Quigley's awake, so while we've got a few minutes alone I want to say however it goes tomorrow... well... it's been nice working with you, kid."

"Gee, Aahz...." I said starting to sit up.

A rough hand interrupted me and pushed me back down.

"Sleep!" Aahz commanded, but there was a gentle note lurking in his gruff tone.

Chapter Twenty-Three:

"Since prehistoric man, no battle has ever gone as planned."

D. GRAEME

We crouched in a grove of small trees on a knoll overlooking the inn, studying our target. The inn was as Quigley had described it, an isolated two-story building with an attached stable squatting by a road overgrown with weeds. If Isstvan was relying on transients to support his business, he was in trouble, except we knew he was doing no such thing. He was mustering his strength to take over the dimensions, and the isolated inn was a perfect base for him to work from.

"Are you sure there are no wards?" Aahz whispered.

He addressed his question to Tanda. She in turn shot me a glance. I gave a small nod of my head.

"Positive," she whispered back.

It was all part of our plan. As far as Quigley was concerned, Tanda was the only one of our group that had any supernatural powers.

"Good," said the demon-hunter. "Demon powers make me uneasy. The less we have to deal with, the better I like it."

"Don't get your hopes up," Aahz commented, not taking his eyes from the inn. "They're there all right. The easier it is to get in, the harder it'll be to get out...and they're making it awfully easy for us to get in."

"I don't like it," said Tanda firmly.

"Neither do I," admitted Aahz. "But things aren't going to get any better, so let's get started. You might as well get into disguise now."

"Right, Aahz," she said.

Neither of them looked at me. In fact Aahz stared directly at Tanda. This kept Quigley's attention on her also, though I must admit it helped that she began to writhe and gyrate wildly. Unobserved, I shut my eyes and got to work.

I was getting pretty good at this disguise game, which was fortunate because I was going to be sorely tested today. With a few masterful strokes, I converted Tanda's lovely features into the dubious face of the Imp Higgens... or rather Higgen's human disguise. This done, I opened my eyes again.

Tanda was still gyrating. It was a pleasant enough sight that I was tempted to prolong it, but we had work to do. I cleared my throat and Tanda acknowledged the signal by stopping.

"How do I look?" she asked proudly.

"Terrific!" I exclaimed with no trace of modesty.

Aahz shot me a dirty look.

"It's uncanny!" Quigley marveled. "How do you do that?"

"Professional secret." Tanda winked at him.

"Off with you!" Aahz commanded. "And you too, Skeeve."

"But Aahz, couldn't I...."

"No you can't. We've discussed it before. This mission's far to dangerous for a lad of your inexperience."

"Oh, all right, Aahz," I said, crestfallen.

"Cheer up, lad," Quigley told me. "Your day will come. If we fail, the mission falls to you."

"I suppose so. Well, good luck...."

I turned to Tanda, but she was already gone, vanished as if the ground had swallowed her up.

"I say!" exclaimed Quigley. "She does move quietly, doesn't she?"

"I told you she could handle herself," Aahz said proudly. "Now it's your turn, Skeeve."

"Right, Aahz!"

I turned to the dragon.

"Stay here, Gleep. I'll be back soon, and until then you do what Aahz says. Understand?"

"Gleep?" said the dragon, cocking his head.

For a minute I thought he was going to ruin everything, but then he turned and slunk to Aahz's side and stood there regarding me with mournful blue eyes.

Everything was ready.

"Well, good-bye. Good luck!" I called, and trudged slowly back over the knoll, hopefully a picture of abject misery.

Once out of sight, however, I turned and began to sprint as fast as I could in a wide circle around the inn.

On the surface, our plan was quite simple. Aahz and Quigley were to give Tanda enough time to circle around the inn and enter it over the stable roof. Then they were to boldly enter the front door. Supposedly this would create a diversion, allowing Tanda to attack Isstvan magically from the rear. I was to wait safely on the knoll until the affair was settled.

In actuality, our plan was a bit more complex. Unbeknownst to Quigley, I was also supposed to circle the inn and find a covert entrance. Then, at the appropriate moment, Tanda and I were to create a magical diversion, allowing Aahz to use the secret weapon he had acquired on Deva.

A gully blocked my path. I took to the air without hesitation and flew over it. I had to be in position in time, or Aahz would have no magical support at all.

Actually magik was quite easy here. The inn was sitting squarely on an intersection of two ground force lines, while a force line in the air passed directly overhead. Whatever happened in the upcoming battle of magik, we wouldn't suffer for a lack of energy.

I wished I knew more about Aahz's secret weapon. He had been doggedly mysterious about it, and neither Tanda or I had been able to pry any information out of him. He had said it had to be used at close range. He had said it couldn't be used while Isstvan was watching him. He had said it was our only hope to beat Isstvan. He had said it was supposed to be a surprise.

Terrific!

Maybe when all this was over I would find a mentor who didn't have a sense of humor.

I slowed my pace. I was coming to the back of the inn now. The brush had grown right up to the wall, which made my approach easy.

I paused and checked for wards again.

Nothing.

Trying to force Aahz's "easy in, hard out" prophecy from my mind, I scanned the upper windows. None of them were open, so I chose the nearest one and levitated to it. Hovering there, I cautiously pushed, then pulled at the frame.

Locked!

Hurriedly, I pulled myself along the wall with my hands to the next window.

Also locked.

It occurred to me it would be ironic if, after all our magikal preparations, we were stopped by something as mundane as a locked window.

To my relief, the next window yielded to my pressure, and in a moment I was standing inside the inn, trying to get my heartbeat under control.

The room I was in was furnished, but vacant. Judging from the dust on the bed, it had been vacant for some time.

I wondered for a moment where demons slept, if they slept at all, then forced the question from my mind. Time was running out and I wasn't in position yet.

I darted silently across the room and tried the door. Unlocked! Getting down on my hands and knees, I eased the door open and crawled through, pushing it shut behind me.

After studying the inn's interior so often in Quigley's dirt sketches, it seemed strange to actually be here. I was on the long side of an L-shaped mezzanine which gave access to the upper story rooms. Peering through the bars of the railing that lined the mezzanine, I could look down into the inn proper.

There were three people currently occupying a table below. I recognized the disguised features of Higgens and Brockhurst as two of them. The third was sitting hunched with his back to me and I couldn't make out his face.

I was debating shifting to another position to get a better view, when a fourth figure entered bearing an enormous tray with a huge jug of wine on it as well as an assortment of dirty flagons.

"This round's on the house, boys!" the figure chortled merrily. "Have one on old Isstvan."

Isstvan! That was Isstvan?

The waddling figure below did not seem to display any of the menacing features I had expected in a would-be ruler of the dimensions.

Quickly I checked him for a magical aura. There was none. It wasn't a disguise. He really looked like that. I studied him carefully.

He was tall, but his stoutness kept his height from being imposing. He had long white hair and a longer white beard which nearly covered his chest with its fullness. His bright eyes were set in a face that seemed to be permanently smiling, and his nose and cheeks were flushed, though whether from drink or laughter I couldn't tell.

This was the dark figure of evil I had been dreading all these weeks? He looked to be exactly what Quigley said he was... a harmless old innkeeper.

A movement at the far end of the mezzanine caught my eye. Tanda! She was crouched behind the railing as I was on the other side of the stairs, and at first I thought I had just seen the movement of her easing into position. Then she looked my way and cautiously waved her hand again, and I realized she was signaling for my attention.

I waved an acknowledgement, which she must have seen, for she stopped signaling and changed to another set of actions. Glancing furtively at the figures below to be sure she wasn't observed, she began a strange pantomine.

First she made several repeated gestures around her forehead, then pointed urgently behind her.

I didn't understand, and shook my head to convey this.

She repeated the gestures more emphatically, and this time I realized she was actually pointing down and behind her. The stables! Something about the stables. But what about the stables?

I considered her first gesture again. She appeared to be stabbing herself in the forehead. Something had hit her in the stables? She had killed something in the stables?

I shook my head again. She bared her teeth at me in frustration.

"Innkeep!"

I jumped a foot at the bellow.

Aahz and Quigley had just walked through the door. Whatever Tanda was trying to tell me would just have to wait. Our attack had begun.

"Two flagons of your best wine...and send someone to see to my unicorn."

Aahz was doing all the talking, of course. It had been agreed that he would take the lead in the conversation. Quigley hadn't been too happy about that, but in the end had consented to speaking only when absolutely necessary.

Their entrance had had surprisingly little impact on the assemblage below. In fact, Isstvan was the only one to even look in their direction.

"Come in. Come in, gentlemen," he smiled, spreading his arms wide in welcome. "We've been expecting you!"

"You have?" blurted Quigley, echoing my thoughts.

"Of course, of course. You shouldn't try to fool old Isstvan." He shook a finger at them in mock sternness. "Word was just brought to us by... oh, I'm sorry. I haven't introduced you to my new purchasing agent yet."

"We've met," came the voice of the hunched figure as he turned to face them.

Frumple!

That's what Tanda had been trying to tell me! The war-unicorn, Quigley's unicorn, was down in the stable. For all our speed, Frumple had gotten here ahead of us.

"Who are you?" asked Quigley, peering at the Deveel.

For some reason this seemed to set Isstvan off into peals of laughter from his eyes. "We are going to have such fun this afternoon!"

He gestured absently and the inn door slammed shut. There was a sudden ripple of dull clunks behind me, and I realized the room doors were locking themselves. We were sealed in! All of us.

"I don't believe I've had such a good time since I made love to my week-dead sister."

Isstvan's voice was still jovial, but it struck an icy note of fear within me. I realized that not only was he a powerful magician, he was quite insane.

Chapter Twenty-Four:

"Ya gotta be subtle!"

M. Hammer

There was a tense, expectant silence as the foursome leaned forward to study their captives. It was as if two song birds had tried to edge through a crowd of vultures to steal a snack only to find they were the intended meal.

I knelt, watching in frozen horror, fully expecting to witness the immediate demise of my two allies.

"Since Frumple's already announced us," Aahz said smoothly, "I guess there's no need to maintain this disguise."

The confident tone of his voice steadied my shattered nerve. We were in it now, and win or lose we'd just have to keep going.

Quickly, I shut my eyes and removed Aahz's Garkin-disguise.

"Aahz!" cried Isstvan in delight. "I should have known it was you."

"He's the one who...." Brockhurst began.

"Do you two know each other?" Frumple asked ignoring the Imp.

"Know each other?" Isstvan chortled. "We're *old* enemies. He and a couple other scalawags nearly destroyed me the last time we met."

"Well it's our turn now, right Isstvan?" smiled Higgens, leisurely reaching for his crossbow.

"Now, now!" said Isstvan, picking the Imp up by his head and shaking him gently. "Mustn't rush things."

"Seems to me," Aahz sneered, "that you're having trouble

144

finding decent allies, Isstvan."

"Oh, Aahz," Isstvan laughed. "Still the sharp tongue, eh?"

"Imps?" Aahz's voice was scornful. "C'mon, Isstvan. Even you can do better than that."

Isstvan sighed and dropped Higgens back in his chair. "Well, one does what one can. Inflation, you know." He shook his head sadly, then brightened again. "Oh you don't know how glad I am to see you, Aahz. I thought I was going to have to wait until we conquered Perv before I got my revenge, and here you just walk in. Now don't you dare pop off before we've settled our score."

"I told you before," Frumple interrupted. "He's lost his powers."

"Powers. Hmph! He never had any powers," Quigley chimed in, baited from his frightened silence at the insult of having been ignored.

"Well, who do we have here?" Isstvan smiled looking at Quigley for the first time. "Have we met?"

"Say Isstvan," interrupted Aahz. "Mind if I have some of that wine? No reason to be barbaric about this."

"Certainly, Aahz" Isstvan waved him forward. "Help yourself."

It was eerie listening to the conversation: apparently civilized and friendly, it had a cat and mouse undercurrent which belied the casual tones.

"Watch him!" Frumple hissed, glaring at Aahz.

"Oh Frumple! You are such a wart," Isstvan scolded. "Why you were the one who assured me that he had lost his powers."

"Well, I think he makes sense," Brockhurst grumbled, rising and backing away as Aahz approached the table. "If you don't mind, Isstvan, I'll watch from over here."

He sat on the bottom steps of the flight of stairs heading up to the mezzanine where Tanda and I were hidden. His tone was conversational, but it was clear he was only waiting for Isstvan's signal to loose him on the helpless pair.

"Oh, you Imps are worse than the Deveels!" Isstvan scowled.

"That's a given," Frumple commented dryly.

"Now look, Frumple...." Higgens began angrily.

"As to who this figure is," Frumple pointed to Quigley ignoring the Imps. "That is Garkin's apprentice. He's the one who's been handling the magik for our Pervert since he lost his powers."

"Really?" asked Isstvan eagerly. "Can you do the cups and balls trick? I love the cups and balls trick."

"I don't understand," mumbled Quigley vacantly, backing away from the assemblage.

Well, if we were ever going to have a diversion, it would have to be now. Closing my eyes, I changed Quigley's features. The obvious choice for his disguise was... me!

"See," said Frumple pointing proudly. "I told you so."

"Throckwoddle!" exclaimed the two Imps simultaneously.

"What?" said Frumple narrowing his eyes suspiciously.

I was ready for them. As the exclamations rose, I changed Quigley again. This time, I gave him Throckwoddle features.

"Why, it is Throckwoddle," cried Isstvan. "Oh that's funny."

"Wait a minute!" Brockhurst hissed. "How could you be Throckwoddle when we turned you into a statue before we caught up with Throckwoddle?"

This set Isstvan off into even greater peals of laughter.

"Stop," he called breathless. "Oh stop. Oh! My ribs hurt. Aahz, you've outdone yourself this time."

"It's nothing really," Aahz acknowledged modestly.

"There's something wrong here!" Frumple declared.

He plunged a hand deep into his robe, never taking his eyes from Quigley. Almost too late I realized what he was doing. He was going for his crystal, the one that let him detect disguises. As the glittering bauble emerged, I swung into action.

A simple levitation, a small flick with my mind, and the crystal popped out of Frumple's grasp and plopped into the wine jug.

"Framitz!" Frumple swore starting to fish for his possession.

"Get your hands out of the wine, Frumple!" Aahz chided slapping his wrist. "You'll get your toy when we finish the jug!"

As if to illustrate his point, he hefted the jug and began refilling the flagons around the table.

"Enough of this insanity!" Quigley exploded.

I winced at the use of the word "insanity," but Isstvan didn't seem to mind. He merely leaned forward to watch Quigley.

"I am neither Skeeve nor Throckwoddle," Quigley continued, "I am Quigley, demon-hunter extraordinair! Let any dispute who dare, and man or demon I'll show him who I am!"

This proved too much for Isstvan, who actually collapsed in laughter.

"Oh he's funny, Aahz," he gasped. "Where did you find this funny man?"

"You sent him to me, remember?" Aahz prompted.

"Why so I did, so I did," Isstvan mused, and even this fact he seemed to find hysterically funny.

The others were not so amused.

"So you're a demon-hunter, eh?" Frumple snarled. "What's your gripe anyway?"

"The offenses of demons are too numerous to list," Quigley

retorted haughtily.

"We aren't going anywhere for a while," Brockhurst chimed in from the stairs. "And neither are you. List us a few of these offenses."

"Well..." began Quigley, "you stole my magik pendant and my magik sword...."

"We don't know anything about a magik pendant." Higgens bristled. "And we gave your so-called magik sword to...."

"What else do demons do?" Frumple interrupted, apparently none too eager to have the discussion turn to swords.

"Well... you bewitched my war unicorn into thinking he's a dragon!" Quigley challenged.

"Your war unicorn is currently tethered in the stable," Higgens stated flatly. "Frumple brought him in."

"My unicorn is tethered outside the door!" Quigley insisted "And he thinks he's a dragon!"

"Your unicorn is tethered in the stable." Higgens barked back. "And we think you're a fruit cake!"

"Gentlemen, Gentlemen," Isstvan managed to hold up his hands despite his laughter. "All this is quite amusing, but... well, will you look at that!"

This last was said in such a tone of wonder that the attention of everyone in the room was immediately drawn to the spot he was looking at.

Suspended in mid-air, not two hand-spans from Isstvan's head, was a small red dart with gold and black fletchings.

"An assassin's dart!" Isstvan marveled, gently plucking the missile from where it was hovering. "Now who would be naughty enough to try to poison me from behind?"

His eyes slowly moved to Brockhurst sitting casually on the stairs.

Brockhurst suddenly realized he was the object of everyone's attention. His eyes widened in fright.

"No! I... Wait! Isstvan!" he half-rose holding out a hand as if to ward off a blow. "I didn't... No! Don't. Glaag!"

This last was said as his hands suddenly flew to his throat and began choking him violently.

"Glaak... eak... urk...."

He fell back on the stairs and began rolling frantically back and forth.

"Isstvan." Higgens began hesitantly. "Normally I wouldn't interfere, but don't you think you should hear what he has to say, first?"

"But I'm not doing anything," Isstvan blinked with hurt innocence.

My eyes flashed to the other end of the mezzanine. Tanda was crouched there, her eyes closed. She seemed to be choking an invisible person on the floor in front of her. With dawning realization, I began to appreciate more and more the subtleties of a trained assassin.

"You aren't doing anything?" Higgens shrilled, "Well, then do something! He's dying!"

I thought for a moment that the ludicrous statement would set Isstvan to laughing again, but not this time.

"Oh," he sighed. "This is all so confusing. Yes, I guess you're right."

He clicked his fingers and Brockhurst stopped thrashing about and began breathing again in long ragged breaths.

"Here, old boy," said Aahz. "Have some wine."

He offered Brockhurst a brimming flagon which the Imp began to gulp gratefully.

"Aahz," Isstvan said sternly. "I don't think you've been honest with us."

"Me?" Aahz asked innocently.

"Even you couldn't have caused this much havoc without assistance. Now where is it coming from?"

He closed his eyes and turned his face toward the ceiling for a moment.

"Aah!" he suddenly proclaimed. "Here it is."

There was a sqawk from the other end of the mezzanine and Tanda was suddenly lifted into view by unseen hands.

"Higgens!" exclaimed Isstvan, "Another one! Well, well, the day is full of surprises."

Tanda held her silence as she was floated down to a chair on a level with the others.

"Now let's see." Isstvan mumbled to himself. "Have we missed anybody?"

I felt the sudden pressure of invisible forces and realized I was next. I tried desperately to think of a disguise, but the only thing that came to mind was Gleep... so I tried it.

"A dragon!" cried Brockhurst as I popped into view.

"Gleep!" I said, rolling my eyes desperately.

"Oh now that's too much," Isstvan pouted. "I want to see who I'm dealing with."

He gave a vacant wave of his hand, and the disguises disappeared... all of them. I was me, Quigley was Quigley, Tanda was Tanda, the Imps were Imps, and the Deveel was a Deveel. Aahz, of course, was Aahz. Apparently a moratorium had been declared on disguises... by a majority of one... Isstvan.

I came floating down to join the others, but my entrance was generally ignored in the other proceedings.

"Tanda!" Isstvan cried enthusiastically. "Well, well. This *is* a reunion, isn't it?"

"Bark at the moon, Isstvan," Tanda snarled defiantly.

Quigley was looking at everyone else with such speed I thought his head would fall off.

"I don't understand!" he whimpered plaintively.

"Shut up, Quigley," Aahz growled. "We'll explain later."

"That's assuming there is a later," Frumple sneered.

I tended to agree with Frumple. The atmosphere in the room no longer had even the semblance of joviality. It was over. We had lost. We were all exposed and captured, and Isstvan was as strong as ever. Whatever Aahz's secret weapon was, it apparently hadn't worked.

"Well, I'm afraid all good things must come to an end," Isstvan sighed, draining his flagon. "Now I'm afraid I'll have to dispose of you."

He sounded genuinely sad, but somehow I couldn't muster any sympathy for his plight.

"Just one question before we begin, Aahz," he asked in surprisingly sane tones.

"What's that?" Aahz responded.

"Why did you do it? I mean, with as feeble a team as this, how did you possibly hope to beat me?"

Isstvan sounded genuinely sincere.

"Well, Isstvan," Aahz drawled, "that's a matter of opinion."

"What's that supposed to mean?" Isstvan asked suspiciously.

"I don't 'hope' we can beat you," Aahz smiled. "I know we can."

"Really?" Isstvan chuckled, "And upon what are you basing your logic."

"Why, I'm basing it on the fact that we've already won," Aahz blinked innocently. "It's all over, Isstvan whether you realize it or not."

Chapter Twenty-Five:

*"Just because you've beaten a sorcerer, doesn't
mean you've beaten a sorcerer."*

TOTH-AAMON

"Aahz," Isstvan said sternly, "there comes a time when even
your humor wears a little thin."

"I'm not kidding, Isstvan," Aahz assured him. "You've lost your
powers. Go ahead, try something. Anything!"

Isstvan hesitated. He closed his eyes.

Nothing happened.

"You see?" Aahz shrugged. "You've lost your powers. All of
them. And don't look to your associates for help. They're all in the
same boat."

"You mean we've really won?" I blurted out, the full impact of
what was transpiring finally starting to sink in.

"That's right, kid."

Aahz suddenly leaned forward and clapped Frumple on the
shoulder.

"Congratulations, Frumple," he exclaimed. "I've got to admit I
didn't think you could do it."

"What?" blinked the Deveel.

"I'm just glad this squares our debt with you," Aahz continued
without pause. "You won't try to back out on it now, will you?"

"Frumple!" Isstvan's voice was dark with menace. "Did you do
this to us?"

"I...I...." Frumple stammered.

"Go ahead, Frumple. Gloat!" Aahz encouraged. "He can't do
anything to you now. Besides, you can teleport out of here anytime

you want."

"No, he can't!" snarled Higgens, and his arm flashed forward. I caught a glimpse of a small ball flying through the air before it exploded against Frumple's forehead in a cloud of purple dust.

"But...." began Frumple, but it was too late. In mid-gesture his limbs became rigid and his face froze. We had another statue on our hands.

"Good move, Higgens," applauded Aahz.

"If it wouldn't be too much trouble, Aahz," interrupted Isstvan. "Could you explain what's going on here?"

"Aah!" said Aahz, "therein lies the story."

"This sounds familiar," Quigley mumbled. I poked him in the ribs with my elbow. We weren't out of this yet.

"It seems that Frumple learned about your plans from Throckwoddle. Apparently he was afraid that if you succeeded in taking over the dimensions, you would implement price controls, thereby putting him out of business as a merchant. You know how those Deveels are."

The Imps snorted. Isstvan nodded thoughtfully.

"Anyway, he decided to try to stop you. To accomplish this, he blackmailed the four of us into assisting him. We were to create a diversion while he effected the actual attack."

"Well, what did he do?" prompted Higgens.

"He drugged the wine!" explained Aahz. "Don't you remember?"

"When?" asked Brockhurst.

"When he dropped that phony crystal into the jug, remember?"

"But he drank from the jug, too!" exclaimed Higgens.

"That's right, but he had taken an antidote in advance," Aahz finished with a flourish.

"So we're stuck here!" Brockhurst spat in disgust.

"You know, Aahz," Isstvan said slowly. "It occurs to me that even if everything happened exactly as you described it, you and your friends here played a fairly large part in the plot."

"You're right, Isstvan," Aahz admitted, "but I'm prepared to offer you a bargain."

"What kind of a bargain?" Isstvan asked suspiciously.

"It's in two parts. First, to clear Tanda and myself from having opposed you in your last bid for power, I can offer transportation for you and your allies out of this dimension."

"Hmm...." said Isstvan. "And the second part?"

"For the second part, I can give you the ultimate vengeance to visit on Frumple here. In exchange, I want your promise you'll bear no grudge against the four of us for our part in today's misfortune."

"Pardon for four in exchange for vengeance on one?" Isstvan grunted. "That doesn't sound like much of a deal."

"I think you're overlooking something, Isstvan," Aahz cautioned.

"What's that?"

"You've lost your powers. That makes it four of us against three of you."

"Look at your four," Brockhurst sneered. "A woman, a half-trained apprentice, a broken down demon-hunter and a Pervert."

"Broken-down?" Quigley scowled.

"Easy, Quigley...and you too, Tanda," Aahz ordered. "Your three are nothing to brag about either, Brockhurst. Two Imps who've lost their powers and a fat madman."

Surprisingly, this seemed to revive Isstvan's humor. The Imps were not amused.

"Now look, Aahz," Higgens began, "if you want a fight...."

"You miss the point entirely, gentlemen," Aahz said soothingly. "I'm trying to avoid a fight. I'm merely trying to point out that if this comes to a fight, you'll lose."

"Not necessarily," Brockhurst bristled.

"Inescapably," Aahz insisted. "Look, if we fight and we win, you lose. On the other hand, if we fight and we lose, you lose."

"How do you figure that?" Higgens asked suspiciously.

"Simple!" said Aahz smugly, "If you kill us, you'll have lost your only way to get out of this dimension. You'll be stuck forever on Klah. By my figuring, that's losing."

"We're in agreement there," Brockhurst mumbled.

"Oh, stop this bickering!" Isstvan interrupted with a chuckle. "Aahz is right as usual. He may have lost a couple of fights, both magical and physical, but I've never heard of anyone out-arguing him.

"Then it's a deal?" Aahz asked.

"It's a deal!" Isstvan said firmly. "As if we had any choice in the matter."

They shook hands ceremoniously.

I noticed the Imps were whispering together and shooting dark glances in our direction. I wondered if a deal with Isstvan was binding on the Imps. I wondered if a handshake was legally binding in a situation such as this. But most of all, I wondered what Aahz had up his sleeve this time.

"Well, Aahz?" Isstvan asked, "Where is this escape clause you promised?"

"Right here!" Aahz said, fishing a familiar object from inside his shirt and tossing it to Isstvan.

"A D-Hopper!" Isstvan cried with delight. "I haven't seen one of these since...."

"What is it?" Higgens interrupted.

Isstvan scowled at him.

"It's our ticket off this dimension," he exclaimed grudgingly.

"How does it work?" Brockhurst asked suspiciously.

"Trust me, gentlemen." Isstvan's distasteful expression gave lie to the joviality of his words. "It works."

He turned to Aahz again.

"Imps!" he mumbled to himself.

"You hired 'em." Aahz commented, unsympathetically.

"So I did. Well, what is this diabolical vengeance you have in mind for Frumple?"

"That's easy," smiled Aahz. "Use the D-Hopper and take him back to Deva."

"Why Deva?" Isstvan asked.

"Because he's been banned from Deva," Higgens answered, the light dawning.

"...and the Deveels are unequaled at meteing out punishment to those who break their laws," Brockhurst finished with an evil smile.

"Why was Frumple banned from Deva?" Tanda whispered to me.

"I don't know," I confided. "Maybe he gave a refund or something."

"I don't believe it," she snorted, "I mean he is a Deveel."

"Aahz," Isstvan smiled, regarding the D-Hopper, "I've always admired your sense of humor. It's even nastier than mine."

"What do you expect from a Pervert?" snorted Brockhurst.

"Watch your mouth, Imp," I snarled.

He was starting to get on my nerves.

"Then it's settled!" Isstvan chortled, clapping his hands together gleefully. "Brockhurst! Higgens! Come gather around Frumple here. We're off to Deva."

"Right now?" asked Brockhurst.

"With...things here so unsettled?" Higgens added, glancing at us again.

"Oh, we won't be long," Isstvan assured them. "There's nothing here we can't come back and pick up later."

"That's true," admitted Brockhurst, staring at me thoughtfully.

"Umm...Isstvan?"

It was Quigley.

"Are you addressing me?" Isstvan asked with mock formality.

"Yes." Quigley looked uncomfortable. "Am I to understand you are all about to depart for some place completely populated with demons?"

"That is correct," Isstvan nodded.

"Could... that is... would you mind if I accompanied you?"

"What?" I exclaimed, genuinely startled. "Why?"

"Well..." Quigley said hesitantly, "if there is one thing I have learned this day, it's that I really know very little about demons."

"Hear, hear!" mumbled Aahz.

"I am undecided as to whether or not to continue in my chosen profession," Quigley continued, "but in any case it behooves me to learn more about demons. What better place could there be for such study than in a land completely populated with demons?"

"Why should we burden ourselves with a demon-hunter of all things?" Brockhurst appealed to Isstvan.

"Maybe we could teach him a few things about demons," Higgens suggested in an overly innocent voice, giving his partner a covert poke in the side.

"What? Hmm... You know, you're right, Higgens." Brockhurst was suddenly smiling again.

"Good!" exclaimed Isstvan. "We'll make a party of it."

"In that case," purred Tanda, "you won't mind if I tag along, too."

"What?" exclaimed Brockhurst.

"Why?" challenged Higgens.

"To help, of course," she smiled. "I want to be there when you teach Quigley about demons. Maybe I can help him learn."

"Wonderful, wonderful," Isstvan beamed, overriding the Imps objections. "The more the merrier. Aahz? Skeeve? Will you be joining us?"

"Not this time, thanks," Aahz replied before I could open my mouth. "The kid here and I have a few things to go over that won't wait."

"Like what?" I asked.

"Shut up, kid," Aahz hissed, then smiled again at the group. "You all run along. We'll be here when you come back."

"We'll be looking forward to it." Brockhurst smiled grimly.

"G'bye, Aahz, Skeeve!" Tanda waved. "I'll look for you next time around."

"But Tanda...." I began.

"Don't worry, lad." Quigley assured me. "I'll make sure nothing happens to her."

Behind him, Tanda shot me a bawdy wink.

"Aahz!" Isstvan chuckled. "I do enjoy your company. We must work together more often."

He adjusted the settings on the D-Hopper and prepared to

trigger it.

"Good-bye, Isstvan." Aahz smiled and waved. "Remember me!" There was a rippling in the air and they were gone. All of them.

"Aahz!" I said urgently. "Did you see how those Imps looked at us?"

"Hmm? Oh. Yeah, kid. I told you they were vicious little creatures."

"But what are we going to do when they get back?"

"Don't worry about it, kid."

"Don't worry about it!" I shrieked. "We've got to...."

"...because they aren't coming back." Aahz finished.

That stopped me.

"But...when they get done on Deva...."

"That's the joke, kid," Aahz grinned at me. "They aren't going to Deva."

Chapter Twenty-Six:

*"A woman, like a good piece of music, should have a
solid end."*

F. SCHUBERT

"They aren't going to Deva?"

I was having a rough time dealing with the concept.

"That's right, kid," Aahz said, pouring himself some more wine.

"But Isstvan set the D-Hopper himself."

"Yeah!" Aahz grinned smugly. "But last night I made one extra
preparation for this sortie. I changed the markings on the dials."

"Then where are they going?"

"Beats me!" Aahz shrugged, taking a deep draught of the wine.
"But I'm betting it'll take 'em a long time to find their way back.
There are a lot of settings on a D-Hopper."

"But what about Tanda and Quigley?"

"Tanda can take care of Quigley," Aahz assured me. "Besides,
she has the powers to pull them out anytime she wants."

"She does?"

"Sure. But she'll probably have a few laughs just tagging along
for a while. Can't say as I blame her. I'd love to see Quigley deal with
a few dimensions myself."

He took another generous gulp of the wine.

"Aahz!" I cried in sudden realization. "The wine!"

"What about it? Oh. don't worry kid," he smiled. "I've already
lost my powers, remember? Besides, you don't think I'd drug my
own wine, do you?"

"You drugged the wine?"

"Yeah. That was my secret weapon. You didn't really believe all that bunk about Frumple, did you?"

"Ahh...of course not," I said, offended.

Actually even though I knew Frumple hadn't done it, I had completely lost track of actually who had done what and to whom.

"Here, kid." Aahz handed me his flagon and picked up the jug. "Have some yourself. You did pretty good this afternoon."

I took the flagon, but somehow couldn't bring myself to drink any.

"What did you put in the wine, anyway?" I asked.

"Joke powder," Aahz replied. "As near as I can tell, it's the same stuff Garkin used on me. You can put it in a drink, sprinkle it over food, or burn it and have your victim inhale the smoke."

I had a sudden flash recollection of the brazier billowing smoke as Aahz materialized.

"What does it do?"

"Weren't you paying attention, kid?" Aahz cocked his head at me. "It takes away your powers."

"Permanently?"

"Of course not!" Aahz scoffed. "Only for a century."

"What's the antidote?"

"There isn't one...at least I couldn't get the stall-proprietor to admit to having one. Maybe when you get a little better with the magik, we'll go back to Deva and beat an answer out of him."

I thought for a few minutes. That seemed to answer all my questions...except one.

"Say...um, Aahz?"

"Yeah, kid?"

"What do we do now?"

"About what?" Aahz asked.

"I mean, what do we do? We've been spending all the time since we met getting ready to fight Isstvan. Well, it's over. Now what do we do?"

"What you do, apprentice," Aahz said sternly, "is devote your time to your magik. You've still got a long way to go before you're even close to Master status. As for me...well, I guess most of my time will be spent teaching you."

He poured a little more wine down his throat.

"Actually, we're in pretty good shape," he stated. "We've got a magik crystal courtesy of Frumple...and that crummy sword if we search his gear."

"And a malfunctioning fire-ring," I prompted.

"Um...." said Aahz. "Actually. I...ahh...well, I gave the ring to Tanda."

"Gave?" I asked. "You *gave* something away?"

Aahz shrugged.

"I'm a soft touch. Ask anybody."

"Hmm...." I said.

"We've, um, also got a war-unicorn if we want to go anywhere," Aahz hastened on, "and that stupid dragon of yours."

"Gleep isn't stupid!" I insisted hotly.

"Okay, okay," Aahz amended, "...your intelligent, personable dragon."

"That's better," I mumbled.

"...Even though it beats me why we'd want to go anyplace," Aahz commented, looking around him. "This place seems sound enough. You'd have some good force lines to play with, and the wine-cellar will be well stocked if I know Isstvan. We could do lots worse for a base of operations."

Another question occurred to me.

"Say, Aahz?"

"Yeah, kid?"

"A few minutes ago you said you wanted to see Quigley when he visited other dimensions...and you seem to have a weak spot for Tanda...."

"Yeah?" Aahz growled. "So?"

"So why didn't you go along with them? You didn't have to get stranded in this dimension."

"Isstvan's a fruitcake," Aahz declared pointedly, "and I don't like Imps. You think I'd like having them for traveling companions?"

"But you said Tanda could travel the dimensions by herself. Couldn't you and she have...."

"All right, all right," interrupted Aahz. "You want me to say it? I stayed here because of you."

"Why?"

"Because you're not up to traveling the dimensions yet. Not until you...."

"I mean, why stay with me at all?"

"Why? Because you're my apprentice! That's why."

Aahz seemed genuinely angry. "We made a deal, remember? You help me against Isstvan and I teach you magik. Well, you did your part and now I'm going to do mine. I'm going to teach you magik if it kills you...or me, which is more probable!"

"Yes, Aahz!" I agreed hastily.

"Besides," he mumbled taking another drink. "I like you."

"Excuse me?" I said. "I didn't quite hear that."

"Then pay attention!" Aahz barked. "I said drink your wine, and give some to that stupid dragon of yours. I will allow you one... count it, one... night of celebration. Then bright and early tomorrow, we start working in earnest."

"Yes, Aahz," I said obediently.

"And kid," Aahz grinned, "don't worry about it being boring. We don't have to go looking for adventure. In our profession, it usually comes looking for us."

I had an ugly feeling he was right.

About the Author:

Robert L. Asprin lives in Ann Arbor, Michigan. He claims he has been a fencing coach, a Mongol warlord, a Klingon, a cost accountant and a deep space mercenary. His first novel, *The Cold Cash War* was released in 1977, and two forthcoming novels await publication, one entitled *The Bug Wars* and the other in collaboration with George Takei of Star Trek fame. This first sally into the field of Sword and Sorcery promises to be to devotees of that genre what gunpowder was to warfare: a new and exciting way of getting the point across...but totally unreliable and impractical.